Totally Bound Publishing books by Carol Lynne:

Kings of Bedlam
The Cut

I0542691

Kings of Bedlam

THE CUT

CAROL LYNNE

The Cut
ISBN # 978-1-78430-987-9
©Copyright Carol Lynne 2016
Cover Art by Posh Gosh ©Copyright January 2016
Interior text design by Claire Siemaszkiewicz
Totally Bound Publishing

This is a work of fiction. All characters, places and events are from the author's imagination and should not be confused with fact. Any resemblance to persons, living or dead, events or places is purely coincidental.

All rights reserved. No part of this publication may be reproduced in any material form, whether by printing, photocopying, scanning or otherwise without the written permission of the publisher, Totally Bound Publishing.

Applications should be addressed in the first instance, in writing, to Totally Bound Publishing. Unauthorised or restricted acts in relation to this publication may result in civil proceedings and/or criminal prosecution.

The author and illustrator have asserted their respective rights under the Copyright Designs and Patents Acts 1988 (as amended) to be identified as the author of this book and illustrator of the artwork.

Published in 2016 by Totally Bound Publishing, Newland House, The Point, Weaver Road, Lincoln, LN6 3QN, United Kingdom.

No part of this book may be reproduced, scanned, or distributed in any printed or electronic form without permission. Please do not participate in or encourage piracy of copyrighted materials in violation of the authors' rights. Purchase only authorised copies.

Totally Bound Publishing is a subsidiary of Totally Entwined Group Limited.

If you purchased this book without a cover you should be aware that this book is stolen property. It was reported as "unsold and destroyed" to the publisher and neither the author nor the publisher has received any payment for this "stripped book".

THE CUT

Dedication

For my dear friends, Lorelie, Kristina and Theresa. I couldn't have written this book without all your help and encouragement.

Prologue

Santana Rogers ducked to avoid the water balloon and laughed. "You'll have to do better than that, Tiny!" She dashed behind the Kings of Bedlam Motorcycle Club garage and waited for another attack. Club picnics were the best. With tons of food, all the soda they could drink and little adult supervision, it was heaven for a girl of fourteen. Unlike most kids her age, the constant sound of gunfire in the background was comforting for her because it meant the men of the club were still busy proving who the best shot was. The competition was a staple of any club gathering and usually happened before the men had too much to drink. Unfortunately, her father had been banned from the contest several years earlier when he'd gotten drunk and had taken a shot at one of the prospects.

"Santana!" her friend, Jaycee, called.

Santana narrowed her eyes and kept her mouth shut. It was just like Tiny to recruit Jaycee to draw her out of hiding. She looked around for somewhere else to hide. *Shit.* With only one option available, she slowly opened the back door of the garage and snuck inside. If her dad,

Smash, caught her in the bike shop, he'd no doubt blister her ass, but Smash was busy drinking and playing horseshoes with his best friend Stake.

She dug a rumpled pack of cigarettes out of her pocket as Jaycee continued to call for her outside. Smoking wasn't something she'd ever tried, but her mom, Ellie, had lost the pack during one of her drunken stupors three nights earlier, and Santana had snatched them up.

"It's just me," Jaycee said through the door. "Let me in."

Santana quickly beckoned her best friend inside. "Where's Tiny?"

Jaycee laughed. "He went to get more balloons." Her eyes rounded when she spotted the cigarette in Santana's hand. "Are you smoking?"

Santana shrugged. "I thought I'd try it."

Jaycee wrinkled her nose. "Gross. No one's gonna want to kiss you with ashtray breath."

Stake was the only man Santana wanted a kiss from, but he still saw her as a child. She'd worn her shortest pair of denim cut-offs and a skimpy halter top, which showed off her tits to perfection, and he still hadn't looked at her like a real woman. "I think I have a few years before I need to worry about being kissed."

Jaycee snorted. "Then you're blind because I've caught Tiny and Gill staring at your boobs today. You could have either one of them with a snap of your fingers."

Santana pulled out a book of matches and lit the cigarette. She coughed several times after her first inhale and shook her head. "Must take some getting used to." She took a deep breath in an attempt to clear her lungs of the burning smoke before addressing Jaycee's comment. "I don't want Tiny or Gill, and you know that. Besides, I know you like Tiny, and I'd never do that to a friend."

Jaycee got all dreamy-eyed. "I do like him. I keep telling myself he's out of my league, but he's so sexy."

Santana concentrated on the cigarette burning in her hand. She refused to point out that Tiny was the only fifteen year old she'd ever seen who already sported a beard. She cringed. She hated beards, especially on a guy only a year older. It was wrong on so many levels, but then Tiny's dad's beard reached almost to his belt buckle. Gross. It looked like long pubic hair attached to his face. "You know I love Tiny, but you need to be careful. That boy's aching to get into someone's pants."

A loud click signaled trouble. "Let's get outta here," Santana said as the big garage door at the front of the building started to go up. She dropped her cigarette and smashed it under her flip flop, hoping she hadn't melted the cheap rubber.

With Jaycee right behind her, Santana ran around the back of the garage to the side. She'd just turned the corner when a big, red water-filled balloon hit her in the chest, drenching her. "Dammit, Tiny!"

Laughing, Tiny got cocky and tossed another balloon up and down in his hand. "I have one more." Before he had a chance to throw it, Gill ran up from behind and nailed Tiny on the back of the head with a yellow balloon.

"Sonofabitch!" Tiny whirled around and threw his remaining weapon at Gill, missing him by a mile.

Gill was Santana's height, which meant he was at least six inches shorter than Tiny. He danced around the yard like a boxer, readying for a fight.

"Really?" Santana sighed. Tiny and Gill were best friends, but lately, whenever they got around girls, there was some weird competition thing going on with them. She chalked it up to raging hormones. Although, it didn't appear to her that Gill had gone through puberty, yet.

"Is the food ready?" Santana asked, hoping to ward off the impending wrestling match.

Gill stopped and nodded. "Yeah, that's what I was coming to tell you guys, but I saw the opportunity and had to take it."

"And you'll pay for it," Tiny warned, smoothing his wet, collar-length blond hair into place.

Santana wrapped her arm around Gill's neck and headed toward the food. "Why do you do that?"

"What? Fuck with Tiny?" Gill shrugged. "'Cuz no one else will, I guess."

Despite their teasing and roaming eyes, Santana loved her friends. A lot of it had to do with growing up with them, but it was also nice to have other people her age from similar backgrounds. She might have been the only one with a drunk for a mother, but they all had badass bikers for fathers. It helped, and she was grateful she had them.

The grouping of picnic tables sat under the cool shade of four tall trees. In south Texas, any shade was good shade, and as she stepped up to the food table, she felt the temperature drop dramatically. She spotted her mom passed out in a lawn chair and shook her head. It wasn't even one in the afternoon, which didn't bode well for the rest of the day.

A large hand grabbed her upper arm and spun her around. "What the hell happened to you?" her dad asked, indicating the soaked top she wore.

She glanced down at herself. She hadn't realized the fabric was clinging to her breasts. At least the material was red so it wasn't transparent when wet. "Sorry, water balloon fight."

"I won't have a whore for a daughter," Smash growled in her face. He shoved her toward the parking lot. "I brought a sweater for your mom to wear later, go get it and put it on."

"It's too hot, Daddy," she pleaded. As soon as the words were out of her mouth, she wished she could suck them back in. She started to duck but wasn't quick enough to avoid the meaty palm that slammed against her cheek.

"Don't you fuckin' ever talk back to me, bitch," he said, spittle dotting her face. "Go get that fuckin' shirt," he slurred. Obviously, her mom wasn't the only one who'd overindulged in the beer cooler.

Embarrassed, Santana covered her stinging cheek with her hand and took off toward the parking lot. Although she always hated her mom, it was only when he was drinking that she felt the same way about her dad. It sucked to love someone and fear them at the same time.

As she passed by other bikers and their families, she tried to avoid eye contact, but she couldn't miss the pity on their faces. She kept telling herself that she only had four more years before she graduated and could move as far away from Broken Ridge, Texas as she could get.

Rounding the front of the clubhouse, she stopped short at the sight in front of her. Stake was leaning against his Harley with a bleached blonde kneeling at his feet, her lips wrapped around the biggest cock Santana had ever seen.

His hands were buried in the woman's hair as he fucked her mouth, heedless of the fact that the gravel under her knees had to hurt.

Blow jobs at the club were nothing new, and it wasn't the first time Santana had caught one of the members taking his pleasure, but it was the first time she'd seen him use a woman.

His head snapped up, and he roughly pushed the blonde back, away from his cock. "What're you doing here, lady bug?"

Still holding her cheek, she pointed to the old Plymouth that barely ran. "Tiny got me wet, so Dad sent me to put on Mom's sweater."

He turned his back on Santana and stuffed his big dick back into his faded jeans as the blonde-haired woman protested. "Get in your car, and get the fuck out of here," he told her.

Santana tried to walk around the pair to retrieve the sweater before her dad came looking for her, but Stake stopped her.

"What happened to your face?" he asked.

She shook her head. "I told Dad it was too hot to wear a sweater." She closed her eyes. "I know it was stupid, you don't have to tell me that."

He sighed and pulled her hand away from her cheek. He ran a finger over the stinging flesh and sighed again. "Bug, you have to be careful around him when he drinks. You know that."

"Yeah, I know," she mumbled. She'd never figure out why Stake and her father were such good friends. What did Stake see in Smash that she'd missed?

"Come here." Stake wrapped his arm around her and walked her back to his bike. He opened one of his saddlebags, removed an old black Harley T-shirt, and handed it to her. "Put this on. It'll be too big, but at least it's cooler than a damn sweater."

Before she realized what she was doing, she lifted the shirt to her nose and inhaled the citrusy scent of his cologne.

"I didn't say it was clean," he said. "But it is my favorite."

"It's fine. Thank you." She pulled the shirt over her head, smiling when it fell almost to her knees. "I could wear this as a dress." She ran her finger over the small rip in the sleeve, wondering how it had happened.

He dug a small metal tin of salve out of his bag. He set it on the bike seat before tenderly brushing her long hair away from her cheek.

"I can't believe you brought that," she said.

He gave her a sad smile. "I've started to carry it with me at all times." He unscrewed the lid and gently started to apply the salve to her cheek. "It kills me when he loses his temper with you, but you need to learn to stay out of his way when he's drinking."

"You're defending him?"

"No." He put the lid back on the tin before wiping his hand on his jeans. "But I'm not always gonna be here. What if I'm on the road and he hurts you worse than this. Who're you gonna go to for help?"

She shrugged. She'd learned a long time ago that Stake was the only one who would stand up for her against her dad. "I never know when something's going to set him off."

He rested his hands on her shoulders and bent down enough to look her in the eyes. "When he's drinking, find somewhere else to go. You live in the country for fuck's sake. Go for a walk or take a blanket and find a nice shade tree." He kissed her forehead. "Just stay away."

"Or, you could take me with you when you have to go on the road," she suggested. All she'd wanted for the last few years was to be the woman on the back of his bike. She wanted to be everything to the man who had come to her rescue on so many occasions.

He grinned. "Can't transport a minor across state lines, bug, but we'll talk about it again when you're older."

She smiled unable to control her emotions around him. "I'll take you up on that."

He winked. "I'm counting on it."

Chapter One

Ten years later

Santana punched the price of the cereal into her calculator and realized she was over her limit. *Shit.* Even the generic brand was too expensive. She glanced at her cart and tried to figure out what she could eliminate. The vitamin supplement drinks for her mother took the biggest chunk of her grocery money, but they were essential. Of course, had their roles been reversed, she knew her mom wouldn't have done the same. Hell, she'd barely registered on her mom's radar as a child.

Squeezing her eyes shut, she fought not to cry. She was so damned tired of going to bed hungry. Of eating cheese sandwiches on expired bread and Hamburger Helper without the hamburger. It was a pity party she had often lately because she knew in her heart she didn't deserve the fucked up life she'd been handed.

With a resigned sigh, she put the corn flakes back on the shelf. *Goodbye, old friend,* she thought as she reached for the canister of generic oatmeal. As a kid, she'd loved it when her mom had made hot oatmeal, but that had been an occasional thing, very occasional, like maybe three times in her entire childhood, but who was counting? It wasn't often her mother had been sober enough to do anything for her only daughter.

She felt eyes on her and turned to see a well-dressed middle-aged woman staring at her. Mrs. Godfrey, her tenth-grade English teacher. She quickly put her head down, causing her long hair to drape in front of the bruise and cut on her cheekbone. *Move on*, she silently commanded, hoping the woman would finish gawking.

"Are you okay?" Mrs. Godfrey asked.

"Fine," Santana replied, putting her cart in motion. She hadn't been fine when she'd begged Mrs. Godfrey for lunch money when she was just a teenager and she wasn't fine now, but people like Mrs. Godfrey never wanted to hear the real truth. She wasn't okay and wouldn't be until the cancer finally took her mom. She stopped suddenly, unable to believe the thought had run through her mind, no matter how unintentional it had been. Her mother was the only reason she was still in Broken Ridge, Texas.

The pain of longing threatened to overwhelm her as she chose a checkout lane and waited. She'd been so close to getting out. She'd even been accepted to the University of Colorado, but that had been almost six years ago. Before her father had been arrested for murder, before the man who'd always frightened her had been sentenced to life in prison. Even then, she wouldn't have put off school if her mother had been able to care for herself. Always a drunk, Ellie Rogers had been in and out of six court-mandated treatment programs since Santana had been a child. Unfortunately, nothing had worked until Ellie had been diagnosed with lung cancer. Even now, weighing barely ninety pounds and confined to her bed, she often used what little strength she had left to rail against Santana because she wouldn't buy her booze. Stupidly—no—naively, she'd hoped her mom would finally notice her once she got sober. Sure, her mom noticed her now, but only as a nursemaid and an object of ridicule.

"Paper or plastic?" Barb, the cashier asked, breaking into Santana's thoughts. She'd visited the store twice a month since the age of twelve, and Barb still didn't acknowledge her any more than she would a stranger who was passing through town.

"Paper." Santana unloaded her meager supply of groceries onto the conveyor belt and held her breath while Barb scanned her items. *Please don't be over fifty dollars* she began to chant in her head. It had happened before, and she'd been forced to go through the humiliating process of putting items back.

She dug three coupons out of her purse. The dollar-fifty she would save on the vitamin drink had allowed her to buy a two-liter bottle of generic grape soda. It was an extravagance, she knew, but it had been so long since she'd purchased something for herself that she couldn't pass it up. She handed the coupons to Barb and waited for the total.

"Forty-nine seventy-three," Barb announced.

Santana pulled out a bundle of wrinkled ones and fives and handed the entire thing to the cashier. "There should be fifty dollars."

With a roll of her eyes, Barb made a production of smoothing the bills before separating them. Finally, after the customer behind Santana cleared her throat, Barb counted the money and finished the transaction. Barb handed Santana twenty-seven cents before dismissing her completely. No, 'have a nice day', no, 'thank you'.

She was used to it. There were definitely three types of people in Broken Ridge. Two of which were those who worked at the nearby state prison and those whose family members were incarcerated. Unfortunately, she belonged in the latter category. Her father had been in and out of prison several times for short stretches, but the last time had been for murder. Even before her father had died in a prison brawl, she'd known she'd never see him again. Not only did her mother have a strict rule about Santana not going near the prison, but also her relationship with her father wasn't a happy one. She wasn't sure what the fight had been about that had ended Smash's life. No doubt, the third category of people in Broken Ridge had something to do with it. Unfortunately, the third type was the bikers of the Kings of Bedlam Motorcycle Club. Why the hell they'd chosen Broken Ridge was anyone's guess, but because they had, she was stuck in the middle of nowhere without a single friend. She should be used to it by now. Growing up, she'd played with the other club kids. It hadn't really been a choice. Since her mother had always been too drunk to watch her, Smash had usually taken her to the club with him when he had business. The club was on a forty-acre piece of land with plenty of room for kids to play and explore without being subjected to the bullshit that went on inside the building. Except for a few quick trips to the bathroom and three lockdowns, she hadn't been allowed in the clubhouse. Lockdowns might sound like one big slumber party, but when dozens of families were cloistered inside a building for days or weeks because of some threat to the club, it sucked after the first day or so.

The non-biker children she'd gone to school with had been told, she assumed by their parents, to stay away from the Kings' kids. She hadn't really minded at the time, she'd had Gill, Jaycee and Tiny to pal around with.

She parked the cart outside the store next to the old rusted Radio Flyer wagon she'd had since she was a kid. After loading the groceries into the wagon, she started the two-mile walk home. It wouldn't have been a big deal except her flip-flop was broken and being held together with plastic tab she'd swiped from the produce department. She prayed the fix would be enough to get her home without having to walk barefoot on the gravel road on which she lived.

As usual, her mind began to wander back to the good old days. The time in her life when she'd had a drunk for a mother, a scary fucker for a dad, three fantastic friends and a crush on a man she'd believed would always be there for her. The Kings had taken everything from her.

The Kings of Bedlam. Just thinking about the motorcycle club made her angry. Her father had joined the club before she'd been born, and had spent close to twenty years doing anything asked of him. He would disappear for weeks at a time before coming home bruised and out-of-sorts, usually smelling like pussy and booze. She still didn't know what had happened the night one of the cops in town was murdered, but it had been the beginning of the end for their family. From that day on, they'd seemed to live in the gray. No one in town would have a thing to do with anyone in her family, including employers. Even her friends from the club had stopped talking to her after her father had been sent to prison for pulling the trigger. And her crush? Yeah, Stake had also checked out of her life.

Smash was an asshole when it came to everyone but his wife and his best friend, but evidently Stake hadn't felt the same, or he wouldn't have turned his back on them after Smash's death. Without her father's income, Santana and her mother had lived on the small government check they received each month. They were the trash of Broken Ridge and she was reminded of that fact every single day that she stepped foot from the house.

Instead of walking along the sidewalk, she veered right and turned into the alley. On the street, she was too much of a target. It would be easy for County Sheriff Gordon to cruise by and spot her. Absently, she lifted a hand to her cheek. One run-in with Pete Gordon a week was more than enough, thank you very much. Gordon was in the Kings' pocket, which made him virtually untouchable.

The wagon hit a rock, jerking her to a halt. Sighing, she kicked the stone out of the way before continuing. "Stupid rock," she mumbled under her breath.

Pete Gordon had to be at least fifty years old. With his receding hairline, potbelly and penchant for chewing tobacco, she still didn't understand why on earth he would think she'd welcome him into her bed. She shivered at the thought of lying under the pig, knowing she wouldn't be able to keep him at bay much longer.

At first she'd tried being polite. When that hadn't worked, she'd just avoided answering the door each time he'd dropped by the house. Both tactics had worked for a while, but Gordon had let her know two nights earlier that he wouldn't be put off any longer. According to him, getting into her pants was inevitable, one way or another, so she might as well accept it. She'd even caught him looking into her bedroom and had been forced to tack one of her bed sheets to the wall above her window to block his view.

Santana exited the alley and turned left down the gravel road that would take her home. She knew Gordon was not only capable of rape but would probably enjoy it more. He seemed like the type to get off on overpowering an opponent, especially when that opponent was a woman. She reached for the hunting knife that had belonged to her father. After the beating, she'd decided to fight back if Gordon ever tried to lay his filthy hands on her again. No one in town would be surprised if she killed the sheriff. Not because they knew about Gordon's perverse nature, but because no one expected any less from a member of the Rogers family. Could she do it? She'd been asking herself that question since pulling the knife out of her father's old trunk.

Once outside of town, she released the handle on the wagon. She dug into her bag for an elastic band and gathered her waist-length dark brown waves into a haphazard bun before pulling off the long-sleeved shirt she'd used to hide the bruises marring her skin. Thankfully, she'd thought to wear a thin tank top underneath or she'd be looking at heatstroke before she arrived home. Using the shirt, she wiped sweat from her face, neck and chest before tossing it on top of the groceries. It was one hundred and ten degrees in the shade, which meant she wouldn't be much cooler once she got home. With no air conditioning, she'd been forced to put the two small fans they owned in her mother's room because when it came right down to it, she loved her mom. Why, she still didn't understand, but she did. *Fuck.*

There were days when she told herself she should call the county health department and let them take care of her mother. It wasn't like her mother had ever lifted a finger to help raise her. Between grieving for a life she hadn't had and drinking, Ellie had barely noticed she had a daughter until her husband had been sent down for murder. Even then, the only thing her mother wanted was Santana to walk into town to pick up her order at the liquor store. Nope, it hadn't been until she'd been diagnosed with cancer that Ellie had needed anything real from her only child.

* * * *

Jakob 'Stake' Wills set his empty beer bottle on the bar and looked around. The clubhouse had turned into a dump. The young recruits had absolutely no respect for the place and it showed in the ripped posters, smell of cum and soured spilled beer. As usual, one of the club bitches was giving Iggy head on the couch. Why the hell Ig didn't do that shit in his room was anyone's guess. Stake wasn't a fucking prude, but, hell, it got old after a while. The whole lifestyle was starting to take its toll on him. It was a hard life, no matter what some people thought. Outsiders believed all they did was ride, drink and fuck, but the fucking and drinking were merely the outlets they used to deal with the real shit.

The mess he'd dealt with in San Antonio was proof of how fucked up things were. The Kings sold weed, pussy and protection, so when Cecil had asked him to make a run to the city to check on business, he'd been surprised to find an entire stable of whores with track marks. He'd immediately demanded to know where they were getting their shit, and one of them, Sweet Penny, had told him it was a new perk of working for the Kings.

Stake had stormed into the house the Kings used for business in the city, to confront his brothers. He found Bones, Jimmy and Rabbit in the middle of what looked like a mother-fucking pharmacy. He would have exploded on the spot had it not been for Hog, the club's Sergeant at Arms, standing in the corner of the room. If Hog was in the house, it meant Cecil knew exactly what was going down in San Antonio. The fact that Cecil was his uncle, and someone he thought he could trust, made it harder to swallow.

"You want another?" Mad Dog, one of the new patches, asked. It was a stupid fucking name, and Stake had told him so on several occasions, but the idiot liked it. Like all biker names, Mad Dog hadn't given the name to himself. The brothers had started calling the kid that when he was a zit-faced prospect because the fucker had got caught pissing on a fire hydrant. Stake had no room to talk. His own nickname was dumber than hell, but his mom had given it to him before he could even walk. He'd been eleven before he'd finally discovered its meaning.

"Stake," Mad Dog prodded. "You want another?"

"No." Stake had planned to confront Cecil, but decided to do it in the weekly meeting they called church. "I gotta get outta here before Iggy blows all over that redhead."

"You're still coming to the wedding, right?" Mad Dog asked after him.

"Free beer?"

Mad Dog nodded. "And food. Corrine's dad is roasting a whole pig in that big smoker he has. Bring a side dish if you want, but it's not necessary."

Despite his sour mood, Stake grinned. "How old're you, twenty-seven, twenty-eight? Why the hell would you tie yourself to one pussy for the rest of your life?"

Mad Dog smiled. "God didn't really bless me in the looks department, so when you find a woman as pretty as my Corrine, who wants you, you know better than to let that shit get away."

"I'll take your word for it," he said as he headed out of the club. He was crossing the parking lot to his bike when Cecil called to him.

"Stake!"

Stake stopped and glanced over his shoulder. He wasn't in the mood for Cecil's bullshit. "What?"

Cecil produced a business-sized white envelope. "I need you to drop this by the Sheriff's house before you disappear again."

"Disappear?" Stake curled his hands into fists. "You think I've been off on a fucking joy ride? You sent me to the city because you knew what I'd fucking find," he accused.

Cecil narrowed his eyes. "I don't know what the hell's up your ass lately, but you'd better fucking dig it out before church tomorrow night."

Stake took two steps toward Cecil, ready to take his frustration out on his prez's face. The last thing he needed was to be reminded about the club meeting like he was a goddamned prospect. He fisted his hands, ready to start some shit when Mad Dog ran out of the building.

"Phone," Mad Dog said, holding up the secured cell phone that was always kept behind the bar.

"Who is it?" Cecil growled without taking his eyes off Stake.

"Hog. He said there's a problem." Mad Dog's gaze swung back and forth between Stake and Cecil. "What should I tell him?"

Cecil slammed the envelope against Stake's chest. "Do what I told you."

"Since when do I do a prospect's job?" He hadn't been Cecil's delivery man for years.

"I need you to feel Gordon out. There's something going on with him, and I want to make sure we can trust him," Cecil replied. "And the next time you question me, I'll put a fucking bullet between your eyes."

Fuck! Stake grabbed the envelope from his uncle. He hated Sheriff Pete Gordon. The fat pig had blackmailed the club for years, and as far as Stake was concerned, it was a waste of good green. "Why don't I just put a bullet in the fucker, instead?"

"Because there'd be someone else to take his place before the last of the shit left his body. The way our luck's gone lately, some pencil-dicked motherfucker who refuses to look the other way would take his place." Cecil jerked the phone out of Mad Dog's hand before turning back toward the club. "Call your mom, and tell her I'm not your goddamned babysitter."

Stake stared after his uncle, thankful that he'd left his gun at home.

"Everything okay between you two?" Mad Dog asked.

Stake chuckled, the sound anything but light. "That's the question of the day."

Mad Dog continued to stare at Stake. "Anything you want to talk about?"

Stake straddled his Harley and settled the half-helmet onto his head before fastening the chinstrap. "Be at church tomorrow night, and you'll get a fucking earful." He pulled out of the club's parking lot and headed toward town. The shit would drive him crazy before he got to say his piece. A conversation he'd had years earlier kept playing through his mind. "Fuck!" He squeezed his eyes shut and screamed into the wind, opening them just in time to avoid a car that had pulled out in front of him.

He zipped around the asshole and flipped the fucker off as he passed. He needed to keep his head straight. There would be plenty of time to chew on the past after he delivered the goddamn money.

The last time he'd made a drop-off at Gordon's place, he'd spotted Santana sunbathing next door. Fuck, even at seventeen she'd had tits that had made his dick hard, which was really fucking sick considering he'd known her since she was four. That had been almost seven years ago, and he'd done his best to stay the hell away from that side of town since, knowing what would happen to him if he gave into his need for the sexy-as-fuck woman he had no business thinking of.

He pulled into Gordon's graveled drive, trying like hell not to notice the house next door. Except for the open windows, the house looked abandoned, complete with a ragged blue tarp stretched over a section of the roof. *Goddamn.* The mere thought of his old friend still had the power to hurt him. Smash's betrayal in telling his bitch of a wife all the club's secrets had prompted Ellie's greed. The fact that the club had agreed to allow the bitch to continue to breathe was only due to Smash's years of service and the innocent daughter he'd left behind when he'd been killed. Stake had used the shit with Smash to convince the rest of the brotherhood that messing in the hard stuff wasn't worth it. He'd fought long and hard to get the fucking heroin and cocaine out of club business, and for years, he'd been proud of the way his brothers had gone against Cecil to agree.

Gordon's front door opened, and the disgusting slob stepped out onto the porch, obviously alerted by the sound of the bike. He rested his hands on his stomach and stared at Stake as if he had no clue why Stake was there.

"Fat fucker," Stake mumbled. Making no move to climb off his bike, he retrieved his ringing phone. *Shit.* "Yeah."

"Why didn't you call and tell me you were back in town?" Rachel asked.

"Now why in the hell would I do that? I've told you a million times, we're done." He hated to get nasty with the daughter of one of his brothers, but Rachel was like a leech that wouldn't let go. He'd been dumb enough to fuck her on three separate drunken occasions and the bitch wouldn't get over it.

"I'm sure my dad wouldn't be very happy if I told him how you used me."

"I didn't use you, bitch. You knew exactly what I was about when I sank my dick in your pussy. So go ahead and tell Magic. I'm sure he'll also be interested to know that you've fucked Tiny and Lumpy in the last six months, too." He was so tired of dealing with bitch drama. What the hell did they expect after a couple nights of hard-core fucking, a marriage proposal?

He climbed off the bike. "Don't call me again." He hung up the phone and shoved it into the pocket of his leather vest, known as a cut, before reaching down the front of his T-shirt for the envelope.

"'Bout time you got here," Gordon bellowed. "I was about to call your boss."

Stake stopped and stared up at the slimy sonofabitch. Although Cecil was club president, no one was his *boss.* Despite what Cecil said, Stake was dying to put the sheriff down and take his chances with the next prick who moved up to take the position. "You'd better shut your fucking mouth before I shoot your ass."

Gordon's eyes went wide. "I don't think you realize who you're talking to."

Stake stepped up on the porch, invading Gordon's space. He towered over the sheriff and narrowed his eyes. "I know exactly who I'm talking to."

A sound from the road drew Stake's attention away from the threat he was about to issue. A slip of a woman with big tits and long dark hair piled on top of her head stopped in front of Gordon's house. "Fuck me."

He blinked again, unable to believe the incredible creature was Santana. He wouldn't have even recognized her if it weren't for those memorable tits and hair. He was too far away to see her eyes but he didn't need to. Kaleidoscope. That's the color he'd always told her they were. She used to argue, insisting they were boring hazel, but he'd never seen hazel eyes with flecks of so many colors in them.

As if she'd been shot, Santana's body jerked before she took off toward the house next door. In her haste to reach the safety of the dilapidated building, the wagon she pulled tipped on its side, spilling its contents onto the hard dry ground.

He shot off the porch before he could stop himself. He didn't put thought behind his action as he ate up the distance between them where she was scrambling in the dirt and gravel to retrieve her groceries. By the time he reached her, Santana's head was bowed as she cradled a bottle of grape soda that had split open and sprayed its contents all over her and the ground.

"Here, let me help," he offered. After righting the wagon, he began to re-bag the groceries. There wasn't enough food in the wagon to keep a bird alive. No wonder she looked so fucking frail.

When he tried to take the bottle out of her hands, she jerked away. "Don't touch me," she growled, looking up to meet his gaze for the first time.

The moment he saw the bruises marring the prettiest face he'd ever seen, his blood ran cold. "What the fuck happened to you?"

Santana got to her feet, still clutching the nearly empty bottle. "Ask your friend," she spat before taking off again.

He stalked toward her. "I don't have friends, so you'll have to be more specific."

She didn't say anything more, but he noticed her glance in Gordon's direction.

"Oh, fuck no." Stake moved to block her path. He reached out and ran his thumb gently over her cheek. "Gordon did this?"

She pulled her head back, breaking the contact between them. "Stop acting as if you give a shit."

Stake looked over his shoulder at Gordon. The thought of the fat bastard touching Santana in any way fueled his rage. "I'd like a verbal confirmation before I kill a man. Are you going to give it to me or not?"

She narrowed those beautiful fucking eyes and dug a sheathed hunting knife out of her purse. "I can take care of myself." She removed the knife from its leather holster and held up the fourteen-inch serrated blade. "I'll go to prison before I let that pig touch me again."

A sick feeling settled in his gut. "Did he rape you?"

"Is that your polite way of asking if I'm still a virgin?" she shot back, squaring her thin shoulders. The action drew his attention to her tits and the fact that her nipples were hard and begging to be pinched and sucked.

"I don't give a fuck if you've had dick up your cunt every day. I want to know if that bastard raped you."

As soon as the words left his mouth, he realized he did give a fuck if men were sticking it to her on a daily basis. *Shit!*

"Not yet, but he tried." She waved the knife again. "That's what this is for."

Stake turned away from Santana and strode toward Gordon. He took the porch steps three at a time and grabbed the sheriff around the neck. Using every ounce of strength he possessed, he slammed Gordon against the side of the house. "What the fuck is wrong with you?" he ground out between clenched teeth.

Without saying a word, Gordon held up his cell phone.

"Stake!" Cecil yelled through the speaker, the sound of his Harley making it hard for Stake to hear him over the deep rumble.

He knocked the phone out of Gordon's hand before kicking it off the porch. "Give me a reason not to kill you, motherfucker."

"So I slapped the bitch," Gordon replied, spittle landing on Stake's chin. "You gonna go against your club and the law for that gash?"

Stake tightened his hold, ready to squeeze the life out of the man who dared raise a hand to Santana, when the sound of Cecil's bike speeding toward him caught his attention. "You fuckin' pussy." He gathered a wad of spit in his mouth before blowing it in Gordon's terrified face.

"Stake," Cecil growled from the foot of the steps. "We don't need this shit," he warned.

Stake continued to hold Gordon in place. He knew what would happen if he went against the club's president, and as sick as he was of the whole fucking lifestyle, he knew it wasn't Gordon's day to die. "You so much as look at her again, and I'll cut your fucking eyes out of your head. Got that?"

Gordon stared up at Stake but made no move to answer.

Stake pulled Gordon forward before slamming him into the house once more. "I said, you got that?"

"I'm the fucking sheriff. I don't answer to you," Gordon replied, obviously feeling safe with Cecil there.

Before he released Gordon, Stake drew back his right hand and drove his knuckles hard against the man's jaw.

Gordon's head flew to the side, nearly knocking him to the floor despite the grip Stake had on his neck.

"Goddammit, Stake!" Cecil bellowed. "You're going to fucking pay for this one on your own dime."

Stake released Gordon and took a step back. He tugged on the chain attached to his wallet while keeping a close eye on Gordon. "Remember what I said." He dropped several hundred-dollar bills at Gordon's feet. "If I have to come back here, nothing's gonna save your ass."

* * * *

Santana watched the exchange between Stake and Gordon through the ripped screen window in her tiny bedroom. She felt her nipples pucker and harden as Stake slammed Gordon against the house for a second time.

"Stake," she whispered to herself. Damn it, why did he have to be the one to stand up for her? For years, she'd tried to put the sexy-as-sin tattooed biker out of her mind, but there he was, in full inked glory. His dark brown hair was a little longer then she remembered, but his big amber-colored eyes were just as dreamy as they'd always been.

She squeezed her legs together at the familiar twinge of need in her pussy. She'd been thirteen, he'd had that effect on her body. Even after he'd turned his back on her after her father went to prison, no other man had invaded her fantasies.

When he released Gordon, she took a step back. The last thing she needed was for Stake to catch her spying. Watching him drop money at Gordon's feet enraged her. How many times had she prayed that Stake cared enough to make sure she and her mom had enough food or money for the electric bill after her father was sent to prison? Smash and Stake had been best friends for years, yet he'd found it easy to forget that fact the minute Smash had been put behind bars.

Halfway down the porch steps, Stake stopped and stared directly at her.

She let the bed sheet fall into place. She didn't have time to think about him. It wouldn't do any good. Like all Kings, he was the enemy.

Chapter Two

Stake sat on his back porch and stared out over the landscape. There wasn't much to look at other than brown grass and stubby trees as far as the eye could see, but that's what he liked most about his place. There was a degree of solitude in the nothingness that he hadn't found anywhere else, and with a blank slate in front of him, his mind had nowhere to go but to the shit he needed to figure out.

Some of his brothers went to the club to get away from their old ladies or children. In his younger days, he'd found a certain amount of peace just hanging with the others, but at some point, he'd changed. He was only thirty-eight, which was still relatively young, even in biker years, but the shit that went down at the clubhouse was getting old. How many rank pussies could a guy fuck before his dick fell off? There were a few bitches who were nice enough to talk to, but other than the occasional blow job when he was desperate, he preferred non-club pussy. The ongoing bullshit with Rachel was proof that if he wanted to find a good woman who wasn't batshit crazy or suffered from stalker-like tendencies, he'd need to look outside the customary snatch.

He reached for his beer. Nope, the club wasn't where he found his peace, it was right where he sat, looking at everything and nothing, and at the moment, all he could think about were those damn kaleidoscope eyes. *Fuck.* After the shit Ellie had pulled after Smash's death, helping Santana in any way would be the same as going against his brothers. It was something Cecil had reminded him of before they'd left Gordon's place, but he couldn't get those damn eyes off his fucking mind.

Despite her bravado, she'd been damned scared of Gordon. Her fear was palpable, like an injured cat curled in the corner, ready to strike at anything that came near her. He didn't blame her. Gordon had let his badge and association with the Kings go to his head, and Stake wouldn't put it past the sonofabitch to go after Santana again just to prove he could. The question was, what was Stake willing to do about it? How far would he go for a woman he wasn't supposed to associate with?

"Christ!" He stood and took another drink of his beer. The sight of Santana clutching that damn broken bottle of grape soda nearly stole his breath. It was as if it had meant everything to her, and from the look of the other groceries, it probably had.

His heavy boot scraped against a nail head, sticking up from the porch floor. Beer in hand, he opened the back door, but stopped himself before walking into the house. He drained his beer in two gulps before stepping inside. Since moving out on his own, he'd adopted a very strict rule about not drinking in the house. Growing up, it wasn't uncommon to see his mom and whatever man she was sharing a bed with passed out on the couch—sometimes dressed, sometimes naked. A beer or two after a long day was fine, but in south Texas, there was never a reason not to have that bottle on the back porch.

When he'd built the two-bedroom cabin, he'd purposely left off the traditional front porch, instead choosing to concentrate on the view behind the house. Front porches were welcoming, and he didn't give a shit about welcoming anyone. In fact, he preferred people left him the fuck alone when he was at home.

After tossing his empty beer bottle in the trash can, he grabbed a hammer out of his toolbox. As he returned the nail in the porch's floor to its rightful place, he couldn't help but think of Santana's roof and that damned blue tarp. Didn't she have a boyfriend or someone who could help her keep up the house? The place had always been a shithole, but from the look of it, he was amazed it was standing at all.

Weighing the hammer in his hand, he considered stopping by and helping out. Although Smash's betrayal had gutted him, Stake knew it wasn't Santana's fault, Ellie's definitely, but no way was that sweet girl guilty of anything.

Tormented by the thought of Santana living in the crappy house next door to Gordon, he swung the hammer and put a quarter-sized dent in the porch floor. "Fuck!"

* * * *

"Come on, Mama, just two drinks, and I'll leave you alone," Santana pleaded. She held the glass to her mom's lips and waited for her to take a sip. The fact that it wouldn't be long before her mom was gone was really starting to sink in. Dr. Braverman had told her that once Ellie stopped eating, she'd only have a matter of weeks. Well, it was the third week of forcing the vitamin drink down her mother several times a day and it was getting harder each time.

Ellie pushed the drink away from her mouth and pressed her lips together.

Santana sat back in the kitchen chair she kept beside her mom's bed. "Oh, Mama."

"Go," Ellie croaked, her voice so dry and weak Santana barely understood her.

How many times had she wished she could do just that? Unfortunately, her heart was stubborn, and no matter how much she wished she didn't love people who were incapable of loving her back, she did. "Can I come back before I go to bed and try again?"

Ellie shook her head in reply.

Trapped somewhere between hurt and pissed, Santana stood. She left the room without turning off the bedside lamp. Yes, it was a childish thing to do, but she allowed herself the satisfaction after the day she'd had. Seeing Stake after so many years had really fucked with her emotions. While her heart sang when he'd run to her aid earlier, the rest of her resented him for witnessing the truth of what her life had been reduced to. It was harder to accept kindness when you knew it could be snatched away at any moment. So, she'd resorted to using the defense she'd honed over the years. She'd never have the strength to physically challenge a man, but she'd sharpened her tongue after years of practicing on those in town who thought to keep her down.

She poured the expensive vitamin drink back into the bottle before moving into the living room. She slid a VHS tape into the old player and settled on the sofa. She'd discovered the tape in her dad's trunk, but hadn't had the guts to watch it. With thoughts of Stake still fresh in her mind, she decided it was time. According to the piece of tape stuck to the side, it was the Kings of Bedlam Fourth of July Picnic. She didn't know what year, but at the moment it didn't matter. All she really wanted was to be reminded of the life she used to have. It had never been perfect, far from it actually, but it had been hers, and she'd felt safe.

Her father had always been mean. In his own way, she assumed he had loved her, but when she'd been young, it had been Stake who'd intervened when Smash had so often punished her. Stake who'd picked her up from wherever she'd run off to and took the time to care for the belt wounds on the backside of her body. Everyone in town knew how far Smash went with his punishments, but Stake had been the only one brave enough to go up against her father after one of his infamous whippings. She'd never understood how a man like Stake could befriend someone like her father.

She supposed she should be grateful he'd been there for her because he'd shown her there were good men in the world. Unfortunately, he'd been so kind she'd believed he was her knight in shining armor who would one day take her away from her parents and Broken Ridge. He'd even given her a special nickname that he'd used whenever she was hurt and he'd come to her rescue. *Lady bug*. She'd told him it was a stupid thing to call a girl, but he'd kissed her forehead and told her she would forever be his lady bug.

"Damn him," she whispered when the camera panned to Stake. Tears filled her eyes as she watched him laugh. The movie had no sound, but she didn't need it to remember the hardy laughter of him in a good mood. She spotted herself in the background. She had to have been around thirteen, maybe fourteen.

Her right hand flew to cover her mouth as she realized her feelings for him had been right there for anyone to see. Had he known? She scrambled onto the floor to sit in front of the television on the threadbare gold rug. Reaching out to the VCR, she paused the tape on a close-up of his face. "Oh," she gasped as she touched the image on the screen. "Stake," she whispered, outlining his chiseled features with the tip of her finger. She grinned when she got to his heavy, black, beard. God, she'd hated that thing. She'd actually told him so at one point, and the next time she'd seen him, he'd been clean shaven. Being a girl with a mad crush, she'd believed he'd rid himself of the facial hair because she'd asked.

Lying back, she stared at him as she unbuttoned her jean shorts and eased the zipper down. It had been a long time since she'd pleasured herself, and with his image in front of her, she slid her middle finger through the light cream of her slit. Moaning, she ran her free hand over her breasts as she turned her attention to her clit. She began to pant as she pressed the heel of her hand against the bundle of nerves, needing to come.

A floorboard on the porch creaked loud enough to get her attention. *Shit.* She lunged for the power button on the television before fumbling with the zipper on her shorts. "Who's out there?" she called, reaching for the knife in her purse.

A handsome face appeared on the other side of the screen door. "I know it's late, but I brought you a few things," Stake said. "I thought about just leaving 'em on the porch, but I saw a posse of coons over by the trashcans."

"A posse?" Despite the very real possibility that he'd seen her pleasuring herself, she couldn't help but smile. She turned her back to him and zipped her shorts while making a production of setting the knife on the coffee table.

"Can I come in?" he asked. "These bags are getting heavy."

She warred with herself for several moments. "Why now?"

"Open the door, lady bug," he ordered.

"Answer my question first." She walked to the door and stared up at him through the screen, pretending the nickname didn't fill her with memories. "Before today, how long's it been since you've been here?"

"You know how long it's been, and you know why." He set the sacks on the porch. "Eat the food or don't. It's up to you." He turned and walked away, the dark night swallowing him almost immediately.

Santana held her breath, waiting for the loud rumble of his Harley. When it didn't come, she unlatched the screen door and stepped out onto the porch. Nothing. No Harley, no vehicle of any kind. Where had he gone, and how had he gotten to her house? "Stake?"

When she received no answer in reply, she glanced down at the sacks of food. She wasn't sure how to feel about the generous gift. Although the help was much needed, it embarrassed her that he knew their circumstances.

"Stake?" she called again before picking up the groceries. The sound of an engine firing up down the road caught her attention. She set the sacks down and hurried to the road, hoping to stop him as he passed by. Why had he parked so far away? The thought of him being ashamed to be seen at her house hurt more than accepting the food he'd delivered. She wasn't sure how it was possible, but she felt even worse about herself and her situation then she had before. It wasn't that she was too proud to accept help, though no one had ever offered, it was the realization that for him, helping her was something to be ashamed of, something to do in the dark of night.

She stood beside the road for longer than she should have. It had been obvious after only a few minutes that he wasn't going to drive by the house, but she couldn't get her feet to move, couldn't accept that he was gone again, and she had no way to contact him.

* * * *

After pouring a small glass of Grape Crush, Santana turned off the lights and retreated to her bedroom. She set the glass beside her makeshift drawing table, intent on returning to the portrait she'd started earlier, before opening the bottom drawer of her dresser. She removed the threadbare Harley T-shirt Stake had loaned her so many years ago. She took off her tank top and pulled the buttery soft cotton shirt over her head. It had long ago lost the smell of his cologne, but that was understandable after wearing the damn thing as a sleep shirt for years.

She sat down at the drawing table and took a drink before concentrating on the portrait. It was a black charcoal drawing of Stake, which wasn't surprising. She'd drawn quite a few charcoals of the sexy biker over the years. Actually, she rarely drew anything else.

She added the fine lines at the corners of his eyes that she'd noticed earlier in the day. She liked the addition to his face even if she was still angry with him. Whether or not he was a good man, he was still drop-dead gorgeous and one of her favorite subjects to draw. She thought of the way he'd looked at her through the screen door. She wasn't sure how to describe the expression on his face. It hadn't been anger, despite the way he'd left. Finished with the eyes, she stared at the updated piece. Although it wasn't nearly as good as looking at the real thing, it was safer.

"What am I doing?"

Before she could stop herself, she crumpled the drawing in her hands. It had taken years to get over him. The last thing he deserved was her longing. He was a piece of shit biker who had turned his back on his friends because the club had told him to. No, she refused to let herself fall for him again.

She filled the trashcan with every drawing of him she could find. Most of the portraits had been drawn on the brown paper grocery sacks she'd brought home from the store, but a few of her best pictures were on a soft vanilla heavy-weight paper she'd bought herself for Christmas a few years earlier. She held up one of her favorites, a portrait of Smash and Stake sitting under a shade tree in the front yard, drinking beer and laughing. She'd drawn it from an old photograph she'd found in Smash's trunk. It saddened her that a man's entire life could fit into an olive green Army chest, but that was the way of her father. She wondered if there was another trunk in the attic for her mother's meager possessions.

Tears burned her eyes as she sank to the mattress. "Damn it." She hated to cry. Hated feeling weak. "I won't do it," she vowed, wiping the tears from her face. She grabbed the trashcan and stared at the portrait of her father and Stake. *One.* She told herself she wanted something nice to remember her father by as she set the drawing aside. The rest she'd burn in the old barrel beside the shed. She had to destroy them, otherwise, she'd be tempted to dig them out of the trash in the morning.

Mind made up, she strode through the house with the trash can. She felt as if she was on a mission to purge herself of the past as she swiped the box of matches off the old stove. Other than her mother, he was the only thing holding her to Broken Ridge. It was something she hadn't realized until she saw him talking to the sheriff. Hope was a wasted emotion for someone like her, and the sooner she rid herself of it, the better off she'd be.

She dumped the drawings into the rusted barrel before dropping the trashcan to the ground beside her. "This is it," she whispered, striking a match. She stared at the flame on the end of the tiny piece of wood for several heartbeats, willing herself to drop it, when she heard the sound of a stick breaking a few yards away.

"It's illegal to burn trash in this county," Gordon said, reaching out to seize Santana's upper arm. He blew out the match still clutched in her fingers.

Fuck. She tried to pull out of the sheriff's grip. How had she not heard him until he was upon her? "Let go of me."

Gordon tightened his hold, his fingers biting painfully into her flesh. "Not until I get what I came for, bitch," he sneered, spittle flying from his mouth. "If you think you can hide behind that dirty biker, you can think again. I own this fucking county."

She pushed against him with one hand as she raked the other down the side of his face. Her short nails just long enough to mark him.

Gordon howled in pain seconds before knocking her to the ground with a punch to the left side of her face.

She tried to scoot away as he towered over her, blood dripping from two of the scratches on his cheek. She needed to get back to the house, back to the knife. Damn it, why had she left without it? Scrambling to get to her feet, she was knocked down again by his booted foot. Before she could move, he was on top of her, pulling at the front of her thin T-shirt.

"This'll go easier if you don't fight." He managed to rip open her shirt with ease before grabbing one of her breasts. "Fuck. I always knew you had a great set of tits."

Pain shot through her as he squeezed her breasts. *He's going to rape me. God, it's really happening.* She fought back with everything she had, landing a few blows before he slapped her hard.

Tasting blood, she dropped her hands, searching for something, anything on the ground to defend herself with. "You won't get away with this."

"Of course I will. You think anyone in this county will take your word over mine? Besides, if you don't stop fighting me, there won't be enough left of you to question." Gordon sat up to straddle her. He yanked down the zipper on her shorts before shoving his hand inside. "You're wet for me."

She almost vomited, remembering how she'd pleasured herself earlier with thoughts of Stake. Gordon's fat sausage fingers felt nothing like her own. When his attention went to her pussy, she closed her hand around a stick. She would only have one chance at hurting him and a brittle stick wouldn't do anything to that fat gut of his. "Go to hell!" she screamed, thrusting the stick upward toward his body with all her strength.

The stick caught the sheriff in the soft skin under the arm, sinking in almost an inch before hitting bone and breaking in her hand. Although the wound wasn't enough to kill him, it did startle him enough to topple his girth to the side, giving her the room she needed to slide out from under his legs and get to her feet. She took off toward the house with Gordon on her heels.

"You fucking bitch. You're going to pay for that!"

She made it to the front porch before she was shoved hard from behind. Her body flew forward through the screen door as if she weighed nothing at all. Pain shot through her as the splintered door frame scraped against her exposed skin. After landing hard on the living room floor, she tried to scramble to the coffee table.

Gordon grabbed her hair and yanked her backward. "You're dead," he spat, slapping her again. "I'm gettin' some of that pussy. It's up to you whether I do it now or after I kill you."

She knew she'd rather die than suffer him rutting on top of her. She gathered saliva in her mouth and spat in his face. "Then fucking kill me first."

He surprised her by pulling a set of handcuffs out of his back pocket. He dangled them in front of her face. "I think I'd rather hear you scream while I fuck you."

"No!" She kicked at him with her feet while swinging her arms, heedless of the grip he had on her hair. She knew if he managed to get the handcuffs on her, there would be no way to fight him off.

He threw his considerable bulk on top of her, knocking the breath out of her. While she fought to fill her lungs with air, he stretched her arms over her head and snapped the cuffs on her, using the wooden leg of the couch to keep her in place.

Pleased with himself, he sat up and moved to sit on her legs. "I do love a good fight." He noticed the knife for the first time and grinned, picking it up. "Is this what you were after?" He stared at the blade and shook his head before drawing the tip up and down her torso, over one breast then the next.

She felt as if she was looking at someone else's body as thin lines of blood began to ooze from the shallow cuts. She supposed she should be grateful he hadn't applied more pressure, but with her hands and feet bound, she had resigned herself to what was about to happen. It would be a fitting end to her life, and part of her welcomed the defeat.

He set the knife aside. "Patience," he told her. He unzipped his pants and pulled out his fat, stubby cock. "Good things come to those who wait."

She turned her head to the side and squeezed her eyes shut as the sheriff yanked her shorts and underwear down and off. She refused to beg him, refused to do anything but hope the end would soon come.

* * * *

By the time Stake returned home, he was livid. He stalked into the kitchen, grabbed a beer and strode out to the porch. He directed his anger at only one person — himself. What the hell had he been thinking? Did he expect her to welcome him inside after years of turning his back on her? Unfortunately, yes, that's exactly what he'd hoped would happen.

"Stupid sonofabitch." He put the beer to his lips and gulped two big swallows. When he'd started to knock the first time, he'd noticed her on the floor with her hand down her pants. The soft moan that had escaped her plump lips combined with the flush on her cheeks painted an immediate picture of what was going on. Two things had happened in that instant, his cock had gone hard as steel, and he'd hated himself for wanting her. Fuck, he'd known her since she was just a little girl. How could want her so much?

There were too many reasons why he should stay away from her. Not only was she fourteen years younger, but Smash's daughter. Worse, the hard life he'd lived had jaded him irreparably. Even if he managed to get her in his bed, there could be no future for them. The club wouldn't allow it, and he'd pledged his heart and loyalty to the Kings. The last thought brought him up short. Church was in less than twenty-four hours. He should be figuring out what the hell was going on with the drugs in San Antonio instead of fantasizing about being between Santana's legs.

He finished his beer before going back inside. He opened the refrigerator to get another but decided against it. Instead, he slammed the door shut. "Fuck." There was no way he'd be able to concentrate on the club with her on his mind. He shouldn't have left the way he had. He'd been so damn mad at himself and his traitorous body that he hadn't given her the answers she'd deserved.

"Fuck!" he screamed to the ceiling, knowing he should have explained why he'd dropped out of her life the way he had. Before he could talk himself out of it, he jumped back into the old beat-up truck he used for errands and sprayed dirt and gravel as he sped down the drive.

* * * *

Instead of parking down the road like a fucking coward, Stake pulled into the grass-covered driveway. He noticed the broken screen door immediately. His heart thumped hard and fast as he jumped out of the pickup and ran to the porch.

He opened his mouth to call out to her, but his throat seized when he saw her crumpled body on the living room floor. Rage warred with heartbreak at the nude woman curled into a protective ball. He knelt and reached out to the shaking woman. "Santana?"

The moment he touched her, she uncurled her body and lunged at him with that damn knife he'd seen earlier. He grabbed her wrist before the blood-covered blade plunged into his chest. "Santana!"

She pulled against his hold, trying to free herself. Her stare was vacant, but it was her injuries that stole his breath. He wasn't sure what the dried bloody patches hid on her chest and stomach hid but one thing was certain, she needed a doctor.

"It's me, bug," he said. "I need to get you to a doctor."

She went wild, shaking her head and kicking at him. "No cops."

Fuck. He understood her concern, but the only other physician he knew was Doc, an old grizzled member of the club who'd gone crazy while trying to keep US soldiers alive in Vietnam. "Okay, no cops."

"Momma," she whispered. "I heard a noise. I think she's hurt."

"I'll check on Ellie in a minute, but you need me now." He slowly took the knife away from her and laid it out of her reach. He held out his arms, wondering if she'd welcome his comfort and protection. *Please, God, let her accept my help.*

Her gaze went to the knife. "He'll be back," she mumbled without emotion. "He's going to kill me."

"No," he replied. "I will never let him touch you, again. I swear to you, he won't get close enough." He looked at the broken door, wondering if it was Gordon's blood on the knife, and if so, how badly the sheriff was injured. Gordon's death meant absolutely nothing to him, but he didn't want the fuckhead's demise weighing on her heart for the rest of her life. "I'll take care of him, don't you worry."

Santana blinked and turned to stare at him, once again. Her eyes filled with tears. "Why would you do that for me?"

The question threatened what little control he had over his emotions. "Because I should've never let Ellie drive me away in the first place. It's my fault this happened, and I'll make it right."

Fat tears began to trickle down her bruised face as she gazed up at him with confusion. "What did Momma do?"

Tired of the distance between them, he scooted closer and wrapped his arms around her. Her body went rigid, but he didn't—couldn't—let her go. "We'll talk about Ellie later." He kissed the side of her head. "I can call Doc Bailey if you want, but you will see a doctor one way or another."

She clutched the front of his T-shirt. "I said, no cops."

"No, I promise. That's why I'll get Doc Bailey to look you over. He doesn't like cops any more than you do." Truth was, Doc didn't really like anyone except his friend Jack Daniels. Stake prayed the crazy old fuck was sober enough to help her. If not, he'd do what he could to get her cleaned up while the other brothers poured coffee down Doc's throat.

He looked around for something to wrap around her. There was no way in hell he'd carry her into the club naked. When he spotted nothing but her torn clothes, he brushed her tangled hair away from her ear and whispered, "I'm going to check on Ellie now, but I'll be right back."

She nodded but didn't release the hold she had on his shirt. As much as it killed him to do it, he pulled away from her. "Stay here, okay?"

"Not safe," she said, her gaze going back to the knife.

He didn't want to give her the knife, but he understood its importance to her. The decision was made when he saw the sheath hanging halfway out of her purse.

"Hang on." He returned the knife to its leather sheath before handing it to her. "Be careful with this. Okay?"

She clutched the knife to her chest and nodded.

Satisfied that she would be okay for a few minutes, he left the living room. Despite what he'd said to Santana, he didn't give a shit about Ellie or checking on her. All he wanted was to find something to cover Santana. The decision was taken out of his hands when he almost stumbled over Ellie's arm in the darkened hallway.

"Fuck!" he yelled, dropping to his knees. He rolled the emaciated woman onto her back. "Ellie?" He tapped her cheek, hoping to get a reaction, but nothing happened.

"Momma!" Santana cried as she lunged for the prone woman.

Stake hadn't even heard her enter the hallway. He did his best not to notice the way Santana's heavy breasts swayed as she began to shake her mother. It wasn't until his gaze landed on one of the bloody cuts that marred her bronzed skin that he snapped out of his lustful haze. *Fuck, I'm no better than Gordon.*

"Momma, why're you outta bed?" she asked Ellie.

He pressed his fingers against the side of Ellie's neck. His suspicion was confirmed when he felt nothing but the rapidly cooling temperature of the slack-jawed woman. "She's gone, bug."

"No!" she cried out and pressed her cheek against her mother's chest.

Although they would never know why Ellie was out of her bed, he wanted to believe the bitch had heard what was happening to Santana and had tried to help. As far as he knew, it would have been the first time in Ellie's life that she'd put her only child above her own needs.

He pulled a blanket off Ellie's bed and wrapped it around Santana, hoping the smell of her mother would comfort her to some degree. "Let me get Ellie back into bed."

When Santana refused to move, he decided to give her a few minutes alone. He stepped out into the living room and called Cecil. Unfortunately, Ellie's death had made the situation even more complicated, and he would need the help of his brothers.

"Yeah," Cecil answered.

"I've got a situation," Stake began. He stepped out onto the porch and looked toward Gordon's house. There wasn't a single light on in the place, and the sheriff's car wasn't in the drive.

"What've you gotten yourself into now?"

"Gordon beat and raped Santana. I found her about fifteen minutes ago." Just saying the words had his blood boiling once more. He clenched his right hand into a fist as he fought for control. "Evidently Ellie tried to get out of bed to help, but collapsed and died before she could do anything."

"Holy fuck!" Cecil barked.

"I need to bring Santana into the club, but I need your permission first. She needs to see Doc." His attention landed on a dark patch on the rotting floor. He reached in through the broken screen door and turned on the porch light. *Blood.* He didn't know how badly she'd hurt Gordon, but it appeared to be more than a mere scratch.

"Ellie's dead?" Cecil asked.

"Yeah," Stake confirmed, knowing Ellie was the reason the club had turned their back on Santana in the first place.

"Bring Santana in. I'll start a pot of coffee for Doc." Cecil sighed. "What're you going to do about Ellie?"

"I don't know yet, but there's something else you should know." He took a deep breath. He wasn't sure how Cecil was going to react to the news about the sheriff. Although the two men didn't appear to be friends, they had worked together for years. "She managed to inflict at least one knife wound to Gordon before he got away." He couldn't keep the grin off his face as he realized how brave the woman was. "There's blood on the porch." He turned back to the house. "And a pool just inside the front door."

"I'll send someone over to take care of it," Cecil replied, his voice tight with barely suppressed anger.

"Thanks." Stake hung up and shoved the phone back into his pocket. He knew the situation would put the club in the middle of a shitstorm with the sheriff and possibly, the Broken Ridge Police Department. The fact that Cecil was willing to help said a lot about his feelings toward innocents. The Kings had always protected the women and children of the club, but Ellie had made it impossible for the brothers to look after her and Santana after Smash's incarceration and subsequent death.

Stake returned to the bedroom and found Santana sitting up, staring down at her mother, that goddamn knife still clutched to her chest. "Let me get Ellie back to bed. Then, I need to get you to Doc."

"We can't just leave her here." She used the wall to brace herself as she struggled to get to her feet.

It was further proof that he needed to get her out of the house and to the club as soon as possible. "Let me take care of you first. Then we'll figure out what to do about Ellie." He settled Ellie onto her bed and pulled a sheet up over her body. He noticed the bottles of pain pills on the bedside table. "She's not in pain anymore," he reminded Santana.

The comment seemed to help because she nodded, dislodging the blanket enough to remind him of what she'd gone through. Christ, the bruises and bloody streaks fueled his anger once more.

He readjusted the blanket, making sure her breasts were covered before gently lifting her off her feet and into his arms. When she started to protest, he shook his head. "Let me take care of you."

* * * *

Santana rested her cheek against Stake's muscled thigh as they rode down the back roads to the Kings' clubhouse. Each time he hit a pothole, he would brush the back of his hand down her arm and apologize. She didn't have the heart to tell him her entire body felt numb. It seemed to make him feel better to pity her, so she'd let him.

"After Doc examines you, I'll take you to my place. I've got a spare room that you can have for as long as you want it." He began to pet her hair away from her face. "We need to talk at some point soon, before we get to the club, about what happened. Cecil will want to know, and I'd rather be the one to tell him."

She nodded. Despite Stake's familial connection with Cecil, she couldn't stand the man. For reasons she couldn't put her finger on, she didn't trust the prez. Maybe it had been the way the club had treated her father or the way Cecil had often looked at her mother when Smash had still been a member of the club.

Whatever it was, she had no desire to tell the prez what his paid sheriff had done to her.

"Can you tell me?" Stake asked.

She lifted the blanket to cover her face. She was nothing, had been for years, but it had taken Gordon's treatment to solidify her place in the world. "It doesn't matter."

They rode for another minute or so before he let up on the gas and the truck slowed to a stop. "It matters because you matter." He uncovered her face and stared down at her. "As soon as I get you settled, I'm going after that bastard. Do you really believe I'd do that if you meant nothing to me?"

She gazed up at Stake. What could she possibly say that would make him understand? He meant well, she knew he did, but had the attack happened two days earlier, he wouldn't have lifted a finger to help her. The truth hurt. "Why'd you stop coming over when Dad was convicted?"

He released his white-knuckled grip on the steering wheel to rub his face. "Ellie. She blackmailed the club. Told us if we didn't stay far away from both of you, she'd tell the cops everything she knew. We had two choices, kill her or do what she'd asked. It was out of respect for Smash that we chose the second option, but don't you believe for a second that it was easy. I even talked to Smash shortly after he went to prison about her demands. He told me that you needed your mother, and I should do what she asked."

Stunned at the news, Santana broke eye contact and turned her attention to the set of keys dangling from the ignition. She wondered what kind of information her mom had used to blackmail the club. Growing up with Smash as her father, she'd had no illusions of what kind of men her dad hung around with. "So you walked away."

He blew out a ragged breath. "The first year or so, it was hell, not knowing if Ellie was taking care of you. It got so bad, that I began to volunteer for every road trip the club needed to make." He brushed Santana's cheek. "It wasn't easy. I promise you that. You were just a skinny teenager back then, and I saw you as a kid sister or something, but things have changed." He removed his hand. "Fuck. I shouldn't have said that, sorry."

"It's okay," she mumbled. It wasn't, of course, but she didn't dare tell him that she'd continued to fantasize about him long after he'd stopped coming around. "It's been years. I can't expect you to feel the same way about me."

"That's not what I meant," he growled, clearly upset. "You're a woman, and that's how I see you."

Confused, she pushed herself up to a seated position. "I don't understand."

"No, you don't." His cell phone rang, cutting off further conversation. He glanced at the display. "It's Cecil."

She scooted over and leaned against the passenger door, making sure to keep the blanket wrapped tightly around her while still clutching the sheathed knife.

"Yeah," Stake answered. "Shit, what do you want me to do?" He nodded and glanced at her. "Okay. Yeah, no, I understand." He ended the call and shoved the phone back into the pocket of his black leather cut. "Birdie, Hog's wife, called and said Gordon was just brought into the hospital. A Broken Ridge cop spotted him slumped over the wheel at the edge of town. According to Birdie, he's on his way into surgery."

Her hand flew to her mouth. She'd never be sorry for stabbing that fat pig, but the fear of going to prison was enough to steal her breath.

"Cecil thinks it would be best for me to take you to a hospital in San Antonio. Cops in the city won't be as likely to bow down to Gordon."

"No cops. He said he'd kill me if I went to the cops," she argued.

"I know he did, bug, but you need to trust that we can keep you safe." He put the truck in gear and continued down the road.

Santana had little choice but to trust Stake. She had no one else, and she couldn't imagine going up against the county deputies as well as Broken Ridge cops without having some kind of protection.

"Once we tell the hospital why we're there, they'll call the police, and hopefully, they'll bring someone in for you to talk to."

She studied his profile in the faint green glow of the dashboard. She'd been alone for years with no one who gave a damn about her. "I don't need anyone to talk to."

"Of course you do." He reached over without taking his eyes off the road, and placed his hand on her arm.

"People don't..." She stopped herself before she could say more. How could she explain that she'd become so used to being invisible to those around her that any kind attention made her feel anxious? Simply put, people didn't care about people like her. It had been a hard truth to accept, but she had done so years earlier, and the last thing she needed was Stake or the police trying to make her feel otherwise. It wouldn't last anyway, and she'd be back to living her life alone. Better to put an end to his protective instincts.

"Gordon didn't rape me," she said after a moment.

"What're you talking about?"

"He couldn't…" She groaned. It was torture to realize her body wasn't even good enough for a man like the sheriff. "He couldn't get hard." She shook her head.

"Thank fuck," Stake growled.

"So there's no need to take me to the hospital. They won't find anything," she explained.

"You're kidding, right? You're covered in cuts and bruises. It doesn't matter whether or not he stuck his dick in you." He turned off the gravel road onto the county highway that would take them to San Antonio. "He attacked you in your home and you fought back. No judge in the country would fault you for what you did, and that's why we need documented proof of your injuries." He reached across the seat and brushed her cheek with the back of his hand. "Can you tell me exactly what happened? I'm sorry, but Cecil will want to know in case Gordon tries anything."

It was obvious he was going to keep up the protector gig, so she decided to give him what he asked for. "I was getting ready to burn some stuff in the barrel out back when Gordon came out of nowhere. He hit me and knocked me to the ground. That's when he tore my shirt off," she said. The unemotional quality of her own voice as she ticked off the events like a shopping list should have worried her, but the opposite was true. She'd get through this and go on like she always did.

They rode for another minute or so before he prompted her again. "How'd you get inside?"

"I stabbed him with a stick, and I ran," she whispered, hoping the softer tone would hide her indifference. She should be angry or sad or…something, but she felt removed from the night's events, as if they'd happened to someone else.

"And Gordon followed you into the house?" he asked.

"Yes."

"Did he break the door?"

"No. He pushed me through it. Then he handcuffed me to the leg of the couch." She remembered the way he'd used her own knife to cut her. "I think he wanted me to be afraid. To scream." She squeezed her eyes shut. "But he couldn't..." The image of Gordon's flaccid cock came to mind. His anger at his own inability to grow hard seemed to fuel his rage toward her.

"Get hard," Stake added.

"Yeah," she whispered. "He said it was because I disgusted him. He uncuffed me and told me to get on my hands and knees because he couldn't look at my face any longer." She closed her eyes, experiencing the humiliation all over again. "He'd used the knife earlier, and then forgot about it. I moved to my hands and knees like he'd ordered, but instead of waiting for him to hit me again, I grabbed the knife."

Stake made a sound deep in his chest that she didn't understand. Was he angry? Had she been wrong to fight back? "I cut him," she confessed.

"How bad?" he growled again.

Santana flinched and plastered herself against the passenger door. "I don't know." Oh God, what had she done? "They'll arrest me, won't they?"

"Not if I can help it. That's why I'm taking you to San Antonio." He reached over and set his hand on her shoulder. "You did the right thing."

"Did I?" She wasn't sure. She remembered his threats. "He said he was going to kill me whether I let him fuck me or not. I begged him to do it before he touched me. I think that was the wrong thing to say."

"Nothing you did was wrong."

She looked at him. His jaw was clenched and his grip on the steering wheel had grown so tight his knuckles were white. She wondered if he was sorry he'd been the one to find her. "Why'd you come back tonight?"

"Because I needed to apologize for the way I left. I hope you understand why I had to back away before, but Ellie's not around to keep me away now." He held out his hand. "Will you let me back in?"

She stared at the large hand, knowing he was the only person who stood between her and the rest of the world. Without her mom, she had no one. Taking a leap of faith, she put her hand in his. "I still don't understand why you're helping me, but thank you."

"Don't." His throat moved as he swallowed several times before continuing, "Don't thank me. I'm just grateful that you can forgive me enough to let me help."

Chapter Three

The sun was just beginning to peek over the horizon when they pulled to a stop in front of the house. Stake turned off the engine and looked down at Santana, sleeping fitfully with her head on his thigh. By the time she'd finished talking to the doctor, police and rape counselor, she'd worn herself out, and the last thing he wanted was to wake her, but they both needed a shower and a warm bed.

"We're here," he said, brushing her hair away from her face. He barely recognized her delicate features under the bruises. Thankfully, the police had been as disgusted by the sight of her wounds as the hospital staff and had promised to do everything they could to build a case against the sheriff. Because the crime had occurred outside of their jurisdiction, the San Antonio Police Department had contacted the Texas Rangers.

Although Cecil might not have agreed with his decision, Stake had taken off his cut before carrying Santana into the hospital. He loved his club, but he didn't want to draw unwanted attention to it in case the brothers had to step in to deal with Gordon. As it was, the police had eyeballed his ink. Luckily, his T-shirt hid the Kings of Bedlam tattoo that covered his entire back.

With a groan, she sat up. "At your place?"

"Yeah." He climbed out of the truck and went around to open the passenger door. "The yard's uneven, so it'll be easier if I carry you."

She slowly shook her head. "I can walk. Just help me get out, and point me in the right direction."

Fuck, he silently cursed. After her meeting with the rape counselor, she'd seemed distant. She might have given in enough to rest her head on his thigh for the drive home, but she'd barely said two words to him. As her current caregiver, he'd also had a few words with the counselor. He'd been told to be patient with her, but not allow her to shut down.

"Come on," he urged, holding out his hand.

In her borrowed light blue scrubs, she ignored his gesture and clutched Ellie's blanket in her arms. "Are you sure it's okay if I stay with you? It might be better if you took me home."

"I'm not taking you back there. Besides, the cops'll be all over your place processing the crime scene and taking care of your mom's body."

Several tears dripped slowly down her face. "Where will they take her?"

"To the funeral home in town. I told 'em I'd call later today after I had a chance to speak with you." He held his hand out again, hoping Santana would let him help.

"She wanted to be cremated and her ashes sprinkled over Dad's grave, but I'm not sure if they'll allow that."

"Probably not, but I tend to make my own rules." He reached for her. "The faster we get inside, the sooner you can take a bath or a shower, whichever you prefer." Although the knife wounds and scrapes from the door had broken the skin, none of her injuries had required stitches.

"I think a shower first," she replied, bracing her hands on his shoulders.

"Okay." He lifted her out of the truck and set her gently on the ground. "I'll make you something to eat while you do that."

"You don't have to," she argued.

He turned her to face him and wrapped his arms around her waist. "I've never in my life wanted to take care of someone. Until now," he added. "Don't fuckin' push me away."

Her tongue darted out to slide over the split in her lower lip. "I don't know how to let someone take care of me, but I won't push you away."

He pulled her closer and held her for a few moments before kissing her forehead. He didn't know what the hell was happening, but he was too old to second-guess himself. Santana needed to heal physically and emotionally before he could even think of taking it to the next level, and although it might kill him, he'd give her the time.

* * * *

Santana exited the bathroom, wearing a faded Harley T-shirt Stake had loaned her. The hot shower had soothed her aching muscles but had done little to ease her mind. So much had happened in the last twelve hours, and while she should be grieving for her mother, all her thoughts centered on Stake. She assumed that made her a selfish bitch, but she didn't give a fuck. He'd shown her more kindness in a day than she'd received in years.

"You hungry?" he asked from the kitchen doorway.

She wasn't, but how could she say no? "I could eat." She glanced down, wondering if the hem of the T-shirt hit too high on her thighs. "Maybe I should put on some pants first."

"I don't have anything that'll fit you." He turned and headed back into the kitchen. "You used to like my waffles. Hope you still do."

Unable to keep a smile from her face, she nodded. "I haven't had them since you helped Dad get Momma into bed after one of her spells." They'd always called her mother's drunken tirades *spells* for some reason. She supposed it made her dad feel better about the woman he loved, but Santana had always seen them for what they truly were. Ellie had been a mean drunk who'd hated her own daughter and hadn't been afraid to say it when she was at her worst. Between her mother's words and her father's punishments, Santana had never felt safe in her own home.

"Well, sit your sweet ass down, and eat all you want." He opened the refrigerator and withdrew a carton of orange juice.

She eased herself into a chair and stared up at him. "Do you really think I have a sweet ass?"

He dropped into a seat across from her. He didn't say anything while he poured two glasses of orange juice. Setting the carton on the table, he shook his head. "I shouldn't have said that."

"Oh." She took a sip of her juice. She was bruised and swollen. Of course, he hadn't meant it. Lowering her gaze, she stared at the waffle on her plate.

"Fuck," he grumbled and got to his feet. He grabbed his vest off a peg beside the door. "You're tying me into knots." He shrugged into his colors. "I made up the guest room for ya."

"Wait!" She stood, ready to go after him if she needed to. "Where're you going?"

He leaned against the wall and stared at the ceiling. "Your place, I guess. I need to check in with the investigators. I'll pack up your clothes if you want."

She finger-brushed her hair down to cover the bruised side of her face as she resumed her seat. "I'm sorry."

"For what?"

"Putting you on the spot. I didn't mean to—"

"No," he said, cutting her off. "You were attacked last night. *I'm* the one who fucked up. I shouldn't have said something like that to you."

She glanced up from her plate to meet his gaze. "I liked it."

He groaned and pushed away from the wall. "When you're done eating, get some sleep."

The front door slammed shut, and once again, she was alone. Without him sitting across from her, the waffles no longer had the same appeal. Still, she didn't want to hurt his feelings, so she squeezed syrup out of the bottle and dug in.

Each bite reminded her of how much her life had changed in a day. The counselor she'd spoken to at the hospital had tried to warn her that her thoughts and emotions would be all over the place, but she doubted they were supposed to be centered around a sexy biker.

Although the legal term for what Sheriff Gordon did was attempted rape and battery, the only thing that worried her were the physical injuries she'd sustained. The emotional damage that everyone seemed concerned with wasn't an issue for her. At first, she'd thought she was in some kind of shock or denial, but the longer she listened to the counselor, the more confident she was in her own feelings. Gordon was a piece of shit who believed she was nothing but a body to be beaten and used, and while she knew she didn't deserve what he did to her, it hadn't come as a surprise.

It was nothing she could explain to an outside observer, but what Gordon had done to her with his fists and words didn't emotionally feel any different than the way her own parents and the townspeople had treated her most of her life. Sure, physically, Gordon had hurt her, but that was the extent of the situation. It was hard to feel degraded by Gordon's actions when she'd rarely felt little else in her daily life.

Finished with her waffle, she carried her plate to the sink. She wasn't about to follow Stake's instructions and leave the dishes, especially because he had a dishwasher. How lazy did he think she was? It only took ten minutes to completely clean the kitchen and wrap the uneaten waffles in foil.

At the end of a short hallway off the living room were two doors, one open, welcoming her inside, and one closed. With a simple twist of her wrist, she stepped into Stake's bedroom. Sure, she knew it was the wrong thing to do, but she couldn't help herself. The rest of the house was simple, yet clean and comfortable, but the bedroom seemed to tell its own story.

Decorated simply in shades of brown with a few splashes of soft blue to brighten the space, his bedroom was a treasure-trove of memorabilia. She stood in front of a wall of framed photographs. Her hand rose to cover her mouth as she stared at the old pictures. Quite a few of them had Smash in them, and she even found a few of herself when she was a kid. One thing they all had in common were motorcycles. There wasn't a single photo on the wall that didn't prominently display a bike in it. She pulled her attention away from the wall. Models and die-cast motorcycles sat on various shelves throughout the room, while a large ceramic motorcycle was proudly displayed on top of the dresser.

She wandered to a stack of magazines neatly piled in the corner of the room and was unsurprised to find pictures of motorcycles and naked women. She studied several of the women. *Boobs.* Evidently, biker chicks loved to show off their tits and it didn't seem to matter how big, small or perky they were. What was equally obvious was how much he seemed to enjoy the magazines. She glanced down at her covered breasts. Though bruised and sore from Gordon's rough treatment, she'd always felt her tits were her best feature. Still, she doubted she'd ever have the confidence to proudly display them for a group of men.

Stake hadn't seemed affected by the sight of her breasts the previous night, so maybe she was wrong about them. Oddly depressed by the thought, she strode out of his bedroom, shutting the door behind her.

After closing the blinds in the guest room, she pulled back the white comforter and sheet and slid into bed. She closed her eyes and willed herself to stop thinking about whether or not he liked her boobs.

After twenty minutes of worrying, she finally drifted to sleep.

* * * *

Stake tensed as he pulled the Harley to a stop behind a long line of police cars. The local and county cars at the scene didn't sit right with him, and he hoped the Rangers were keeping the yokels from contaminating the evidence. He crossed the yard, intent on talking to the Texas Ranger in charge, but was brought up short by the sound of two of the local cops laughing. *Fucking hell.* Robby Langers and Colton Fellows stood to the right of the porch with their arms crossed over their chests and amused expressions on their faces. "What the hell's so funny?"

Robby stared at Stake's cut and automatically dismissed him. "This so-called crime scene's off limits."

"So-called?" Stake questioned, curling his hands into fists. "What the fuck's that supposed to mean?" He charged toward Robby, but strong arms wrapped around him from behind. "Get the fuck off me!"

"Not until you calm down. Or would you rather I put you in the back of my SUV?" a deep voiced asked.

Stake looked over his shoulder to see a man in a white western-style shirt and a tan Resistol cowboy hat. The man was obviously a Texas Ranger, but he wasn't the same man Stake had spoken to at the hospital. With a simple nod, he relaxed and waited for the Ranger to release him. "I came by to pick up Santana's clothes and to make sure the funeral home had been here."

"You're Jakob Wills?"

"Yeah, and you are?" Stake wasn't about to shake the man's hand, at least not until he was sure he was on the right side of the crime that had occurred.

"Bob Thatcher. Jack told me you'd be by."

"Where is Jack?" Stake liked the Ranger he'd met at the hospital better than the douche who'd kept him from rearranging Robby's smug face.

"Out back where the alleged attack was initiated," Thatcher replied.

With his hands still fisted, Stake put space between himself and the Ranger before he ended up in jail. He started to argue with Thatcher, but decided it would be better to find Jack and see what the hell was going on. Turning away from the trio, he stalked around the house. He spotted Jack Boone holding a stack of papers. "Hey."

Jack spun around. "This is a crime scene. You're not allowed to be here."

At least one of the cops on hand acknowledged a crime had taken place. "I came to get some clothes for Santana, and to make sure the funeral home picked up Ellie."

Jack nodded. "They were here first thing." He held up the papers. "Is there something you haven't told me?"

Stake stared at the portrait of himself. He held out his hand. "Can I see those?"

Jack glanced at the crime scene photographer who was busy snapping pictures of Santana's torn and discarded clothes. "I'd better not. I don't want to compromise the case, but in case you're wondering, they're all of you."

"Where'd you find them?" Stake asked, his gaze going from the picture of himself and the torn Harley T-shirt on the ground. He recognized the shirt immediately as his old favorite, the one he'd loaned Santana and had never gotten back. The small tear in the sleeve where he'd gotten caught up on a barbed wire fence confirmed it was his. Of all the clothes she had, why had she been wearing that particular shirt?

Jack gestured to the blackened barrel. "According to her statement, Santana was out here burning trash."

The stack of drawings was a thick one, so Santana must've been working on them for a long time. Why had she drawn them, and more important, what made her decide to burn them? Stake rubbed the back of his neck. "Can I have those once you're done with them?"

Jack shrugged. "Could be a while, but trash is usually public property, so I guess so." He narrowed his eyes.

"Do you have any idea why she seems obsessed with you? I thought the two of you were friends."

They weren't friends, but they weren't anything more than that, either. How could Stake tell the Ranger he'd turned his back on Santana years earlier and not come off like the biggest asshole in the state of Texas? "I've known her for years. I was her dad's best friend."

Jack's eyebrows rose. "Then I'd say she's had the crush for a long time."

"Yeah, maybe you're right." He glanced at the T-shirt again. The realization seared through Stake. He needed to talk to her. "Can I get some of her clothes?" If he had to see her walk around his house in nothing but his T-shirts, he wouldn't be able to keep his hands to himself.

"You still have my business card?" Jack asked.

"Sure."

"Call me tomorrow, and I'll let you know if we've finished up here. Until then, I can't let you into the house."

Fuck. Stake wasn't sure how he'd control himself, but he'd put a padlock on his zipper if he had to.

* * * *

Santana woke with a start, sitting straight up in bed. The room was dark, and it took her a moment to remember where she was. She glanced at the bedside clock and couldn't believe it was almost nine p.m. How had she slept for over twelve hours? It didn't seem possible. Stranger yet, why hadn't Stake been in to wake her?

She threw back the covers and swung her legs over the side of the bed, pleased that some of the soreness in her muscles had melted away while she'd slept. Pulling the hem of the borrowed T-shirt down, she made her way from the room. His door was still closed, but she wasn't sure if that meant he was sleeping or hadn't returned home. Wandering into the living room, she immediately noticed him stretched out on the deep leather sofa.

"I thought you might sleep through 'til morning," he said without opening his eyes.

Her pussy clenched at the scratchy sound of his deep voice.

"Did you talk to the funeral home?" she asked, sitting on the coffee table beside him.

He stretched his muscular arms over his head and opened his eyes to stare over at her. "Yeah. They're going to go ahead and cremate her on Friday. They asked about a memorial service, but I told them I'd have to discuss it with you." He sat up and did his best to tame his wild, shoulder-length hair.

"No, no service." She felt tears sting her eyes. "If you'll drive me, I'd like to have something on my own at Dad's grave."

"Of course I will."

When his gaze traveled to her bare legs, her nipples hardened. *Christ.* Without thinking, she squeezed her thighs together to ease the ache in her pussy.

He grunted. "Answer a question."

"Okay."

He scooted to the edge of the couch, bracketing her legs with his. "Why'd you throw pictures of me away?"

Fuck. Fuck. Fuck. She stood, intending to get away from him before he saw the truth in her eyes.

He reached out and grabbed her wrist, keeping her between his thighs. "Answer me, goddammit."

Held in place, she stared at the wall over his head. "Because I realized how unhealthy it was to keep them around."

"Unhealthy for who?"

She shook her head. She couldn't do this. "Please let me go. I've been humiliated enough, don't you think?"

Still holding her wrist, he stood, putting his body in direct contact with hers. "I won't push it for now, but you'll eventually tell me." He released her wrist and wrapped his arms around her waist. "We have a lot of things to talk about once you're feeling better. Like why you were wearing my Harley shirt when Gordon attacked you."

She couldn't help herself. She rested her cheek against his chest for just a moment before pulling away. "I think you mean once I'm looking better, because other than a slight throb in my eye, I'm fine."

Stake cupped her face between his big hands and tilted her head back until their eyes met. "Even bruised, you're more beautiful than any woman I've ever known."

"Yeah, right. I remember the women who used to hang all over you." She didn't mention how jealous she'd always been of the big-titted sluts.

"Do you? Because I don't. I've had bitches in my bed since I was fourteen, and I don't remember a fuckin' thing about any of them." He ran his thumb over Santana's lower lip, avoiding the healing split. "I want you so bad I can't stand it."

She touched the tip of her tongue to his thumb. She had no idea why he'd want her, but she'd thought of nothing else for years. "Then take me," she whispered.

He leaned down and brushed his lips over her mouth. "Someday, but not yet."

Chapter Four

Stake heard the backdoor open behind him just as he ended the call with Jack. "They're finally done with your house, so I'll run over and pack up your clothes," he told Santana.

"Can I go?" she asked.

"I don't think that's a good idea." He shoved his phone into his back pocket before turning around to face her. "I don't mind doing it."

She tucked her long dark hair behind her ears. "I think Momma had a black dress in her closet. I want to see if it fits, so I can wear it when we go to the cemetery."

"I'll buy ya a black dress." He'd called Cecil to see if either Mad Dog or Hog could meet him at Santana's, but Cecil had given him a bullshit excuse about how it would be best for the club if they kept their distance from the crime scene. It was fucked up because Stake didn't trust himself not to kill Gordon if he saw him.

She crossed her arms, drawing his attention to her large tits. "Maybe I don't want you going through my things."

"Tough shit." He decided to tell her the truth. "Gordon's being released today, and I don't want you anywhere near him."

The color drained from her gorgeous face. "It's been less than three days. How's he getting out?"

"Evidently, his injuries were more superficial then they led us to believe." He moved to wrap his arms around her. "I won't let him hurt you again. If the cops don't do their job, believe me, I'll take care of Gordon myself." It was the way he'd wanted it in the first place. The only reason he'd gone along with Cecil's demand to take Santana to the hospital was to keep her from getting into trouble with the law.

"No." She rested her cheek on his chest. It was something she'd done on several occasions and each time, it filled him with a sense of warmth he'd never felt before. "I lost my dad that way—I won't lose you, too."

He held her tighter. "What kind of man would I be if I let Gordon get away with what he did to you? If it means going to prison, I'll pay the price."

"And leave me alone, just like Smash did, to fend for myself?" She pushed against his chest until he released her. "No. I can't go through that again. I'll kill him myself before I let you do something like that for me."

No way in hell would he let his woman do his job. Stake stilled, realizing he'd already begun to think of her as his. He watched her pace around the back porch, the T-shirt barely covering her bare ass, and knew in his gut, she was his woman. He dug his phone out and looked at the time. If they hurried, they could be in and out of her house before nine. Surely, the hospital wouldn't release Gordon that early. "Let's go."

She smiled and jumped off the side of the porch to the dirt below. "Are we taking the bike?"

He would love nothing more than to feel her wrapped around his back, but it wasn't possible. "I'd like to get everything out of the house that you're going to need for the next few months. Can't do that with the bike." He opened the passenger door of the old truck and waited for her to get in before going around to climb behind the steering wheel.

"Can we take the bike to the cemetery once we get Momma's ashes? I think Dad would appreciate that."

"Sure." He kept his eyes on the road and off the bared legs beside him. For three days, those fucking legs had teased him. Although he'd seen her naked on the night of the attack, he hadn't been in the position to truly worship her body the way it deserved. He wanted to touch and lick every inch of her sun-bronzed skin while she moaned underneath him. *Fuck.* He released the steering wheel and dropped his right hand to his lap in an attempt to hide his erection. Not to brag, but he was a big man, and when his body decided to respond sexually, there was no way in hell to successfully hide it.

"Stake?"

"Yeah?" He waited for her to continue. When she didn't, he glanced her way.

"How long before I heal enough?" she asked.

Since he hadn't seen her wounds since the first night, he wasn't sure how to answer. He returned his attention to the gravel road. "I don't know. Bruises can take a while to disappear completely, but the swelling is pretty much gone already. Why? Are you hurting?"

She shook her head. "Because I want you to touch me, and you said I needed to heal first."

"Fuck, baby," he groaned. "It's not your body I'm worried about. I thought I made that clear. I just don't want to push the physical stuff until I know you're ready for it. Freaking you out isn't something I'm willing to do."

Again, silence greeted him. He wasn't sure what else to say, so he kept his mouth shut and wondered if he'd ever understand Santana's moods.

* * * *

After packing her own clothes, Santana started on her mom's closet. Although they wore the same size, they'd always had very different tastes. Ellie had dressed for Smash, but Santana didn't have anyone to impress, so she chose to be comfortable. She glanced down at her old ratty jean shorts. Yep, comfort.

"So what's up with the blue tarp on the roof?" Stake asked from the bedroom doorway.

Her hand closed around the black dress she'd been looking for. "The roof leaks." *Duh.*

"I figured that much, but why haven't you hired someone to fix it?"

"We tried. A few years ago, Mom gave me permission to sell Dad's bike so we could have the roof replaced. The guys who were going to do it said they needed half the money up front to buy supplies. Unfortunately, they never came back to do the work." It had been an expensive lesson, but one that she'd never forget.

"That's bullshit. Did you report them?"

"Tried, but the cops said they couldn't do anything since I didn't have a contract." She held the dress in front of her and studied herself in the mirror. The jersey dress was short, but at least the neckline wasn't as low as some of the other dresses and shirts in her mom's closet. "Anyway, that's the last time I trusted anyone in this town."

Stake stepped into the room and leaned against the wall beside the closet. "You trust me," he pointed out.

"Mostly." She didn't want to hurt his feelings, but she wasn't positive that she truly trusted him. Not that it was the same, but she supposed she felt closer to him than anyone. However, even though he had been nothing but kind, she knew she couldn't count on him to stick around. He'd left before, and once he realized how fucked up she was, he'd probably leave again. Funny, she was fucked up because she wasn't fucked up over what happened with Gordon. She might be withdrawn, but she wasn't stupid. Any other woman who'd been through what Gordon had done to her would be traumatized. What exactly did it say about her that she didn't feel what everyone expected her to feel?

In an attempt to change the subject, she held the dress up. "I need to try this on."

He shook his head and moved to pull several dresses, skirts and blouses from Ellie's closet. "You'll have to take these with us. I want to be long gone before they release Gordon."

Santana studied the dress in her hand. She had much bigger breasts than her mom, but she didn't have anything else that would be appropriate for a funeral. Perhaps Stake knew she didn't have anything that looked nice. Maybe that's why he'd pulled the clothes from her mom's closet. "Okay."

"Is there anything else in here you want to take with us?" he asked.

"Yeah." She handed the dress to him before gathering several photos from her mom's dresser. She stared down at the simple thin gold band that sat on the bedside table and suddenly felt guilty that her mom hadn't been wearing it when they took her away. The ring hadn't fit for months, but Ellie always insisted it be within sight of the bed. Santana scooped it up and shoved it into the pocket of her shorts.

"I think that's all." She glanced at Stake. "We'll come back here again, won't we?"

"Sure. After we settle the situation with Gordon and the cops, we'll come back." He took the pictures from her and left the room.

Before joining him, she ducked back into her bedroom. She wasn't sure why she felt sad at the thought of leaving the house. The air conditioning didn't work, the roof leaked and she'd had more beatings than hugs in the place, but it had been the only home she'd ever known.

* * * *

Stake filled a galvanized bucket with ice and bottle of beer before retrieving the marinated steaks from the refrigerator. "I thought we could eat outside on the porch if that's okay?"

"Sure." Santana paused in the process of stirring her homemade potato salad.

He nodded toward the living room. "There's a tablecloth in the linen closet."

"Okay. I'll find it, and be out in a minute."

Carrying the bucket and platter of meat, he returned to the back porch. He'd spent the majority of the day, since returning from Santana's house, hiding on the porch or in the garage. It was a cowardly thing to do, and he knew it. But, damn, the constant need for restraint was wearing on him.

The door opened, and he turned to watch Santana shake out the tablecloth. Despite his best intentions, he couldn't take his eyes off her tits. Goddamn, those things were big, beautiful and just begging for his mouth.

She cleared her throat as she reached for the hem of her tight T-shirt. "I'll be happy to give you a closer look."

Before he could force out a token protest, she pulled her shirt over her head. Wearing nothing but a pair of short denim shorts and a simple white bra, her body left him speechless. He made a mental note to buy her some girly underwear next time he rode into the city, not that she needed it to look sexy, because *fuck*. He shook his head and rubbed the back of his neck. Those tits deserved to be covered by the finest lace money could buy.

"Tell me you're ready for this." He tried to keep the pleading out of his voice, but knew he'd failed miserably. For days, he'd tried to put his finger on what it was about Santana that drew him to her. She'd needed him like no one ever had, and he'd be a liar if he said it didn't make him feel special. No one had ever looked at him the way she did. Sure, he was used to expressions of fear or lust on people's faces when they saw him, but she gazed at him as if he genuinely mattered to her. It was a heady feeling.

"I've been waiting for years for you to notice me," she confessed. She reached behind her back and unfastened her bra but didn't shrug out of it. Instead, she held her hands in front of her. "That being said, I think I'm the one who should ask if you're ready for this?"

He closed the distance between them and pulled her roughly against his chest. He took her mouth in a savage kiss, thrusting his tongue deep as he fought like hell against his body's needs. Christ. If he took her to bed, would she end up resenting him for it?

She put enough space between them to drop her bra to the porch floor, leaving her bare tits unencumbered.

"Fuck, bug, what're you doing to me?" he asked as he reached to cup her breasts. *Perfect.* She was so fucking perfect that her bountiful breasts overflowed his hands. He'd been with other women with big tits, but there was a huge difference between fake and the real thing, and goddamned if Santana's weren't the real thing.

He blindly used his foot to hook the leg of one of the outdoor chairs and pulled it close enough to sit. The new position put her puckered nipples at the perfect height for his mouth. "It's sick how often I've thought about these."

She buried her fingers in his hair as he swirled his tongue around the dark pink, eraser-sized nipple. He flicked the pebbled nub with the tip of his tongue before latching on. *Oh, fuck.* The taste of her skin was everything he'd known it would be. He drew the nipple into his mouth and sucked, his cock throbbing with each moan that erupted from her delicate throat.

Before he could stop himself, his hands went to the zipper of her barely there denim shorts. "Need to taste that sweet pussy," he panted, releasing her nipple.

"Please." She pushed her shorts down before climbing on top of the table.

Still seated, he insinuated himself between her spread thighs, unable to tear his gaze away from the prettiest pussy ever created. "Fuck, bug. Goddamn. I want to crawl inside your cunt and eat you from the inside out."

Stake nearly came in his jeans when she reached between her legs and spread the lips of her pussy. "Touch me," she begged.

It took one swipe of her clit with his tongue to know he was forever hooked. *Christ.* He lapped up her sweet juices while he fumbled to get his jeans open.

The crunching sound of tires on the gravel driveway felt like a bucket of cold water being poured over him. He stood so fast, the chair fell to the ground. "Get into the house," he ordered, helping Santana from the table. "Don't come out unless I call for you."

"Who is it?" she asked, gathering her clothes.

"I don't know." He zipped his jeans but left his shirt lying on the porch. Whoever the fuck had interrupted better have a damn good reason. He walked Santana to the door and opened it for her before giving her a deep kiss. "Go on. I'll get rid of them."

She nodded before ducking inside.

"Back here," he called, taking the burned meat off the grill.

"Evening," Jack said, rounding the side of the house. He was followed closely by the asshole Ranger Stake had met at Santana's.

"What's up?" Stake asked.

Jack shook his head in sympathy as he stared at the inedible steaks. "We came by to question Santana Rogers, again."

"Why?" Stake crossed his arms over his bare chest. No way in the fucking world did he want her to relive that night again.

"Conflicting stories on what happened the night of the stabbing," Jack replied.

"You mean the night of the attack," Stake corrected.

Jack nodded his head, acknowledging the difference. "I know she's been through a rough ordeal, but I need Santana to answer his charges."

"She's already told you exactly what happened," Stake reminded the Ranger.

"Yes, but it's not a cut and dry case, so I need all the help she can give me. I thought maybe she'd remembered something else since that night." Jack resettled his cowboy hat. "Would you please bring her out here?"

"Come on out here, bug," he said without the need to raise his voice. He knew she'd been listening on the other side of the door. "Upset her, and we're gonna have a problem," he warned the two Rangers.

"Is that a threat?" Thatcher, the other Ranger took a step forward.

Jack held up his hand to silence his partner. "Just a few questions."

The backdoor opened, and Santana stepped out of the house, her clothes in place, sans bra. Stake's gaze went straight to the tits he'd enjoyed only moments earlier. "What kind of information do you need from me?" Santana asked, moving to stand at Stake's side.

He wrapped his arm protectively around her waist and pulled her closer.

Jack sighed and looked out over the barren landscape. "Gordon claims there was absolutely no attempted rape involved in the altercation between the two of you. I'm hoping you can give me evidence otherwise."

"Like what?" Santana asked.

Stake felt her slight tremble and wanted to put an end to the interrogation, but knew the law wasn't on his side, never had been.

"Pete Gordon claims he went over to your place to tell you that it was against the law to burn garbage and you went crazy and stabbed him with a stick. According to him, he had to hit you to get you to release your hold on the weapon. That's when you ran into the house, and when he went after you with plans to arrest you for assault, you stabbed him."

Stake stared at the Texas Ranger, trying to determine whether or not the man actually believed Gordon's story.

"That's bullshit!" Santana yelled. "I hadn't burned anything when he attacked me. Are you honestly going to believe he was hiding in the shadows of my backyard just waiting for me to set fire to something?" She shook her head. "That right there should tell you he's a lying sonofabitch."

Jack cleared his throat and flipped through his notebook. "Any distinguishing marks on the lower half of his body that you could identify?"

"You mean other than that stubby cock of his that couldn't get hard?" she asked.

"Yes, ma'am," Jack replied, clearly uneasy.

"No. I tried not to look at the thing." Santana stared up at Stake with tears in her eyes. "He's going to get away with it, isn't he?"

Stake knew better, but he held his tongue. Instead, he bent and gave her a deep kiss he hoped would comfort her. There were many ways to punish a man, and eventually, Gordon would be sorry he didn't choose jail time as his option.

"What about the cuts on your chest. You claim Gordon cut you with your own knife. Is that still the way you remember it?" Jack asked.

Santana nodded.

Jack tore his hat off his head and thumped it against his leg. "Ma'am, the only fingerprints on the knife you turned over to me at the hospital belong to you and Mr. Wills. Our technicians haven't found a single print on that knife belonging to Pete Gordon."

Santana buried her face against Stake's chest.

He wrapped both arms around her and leaned his rested his chin on the top of her head. "So, what now?"

"We'll continue to investigate, but at this point, if we were forced to arrest someone, it would probably be Miss Rogers."

"We came to you for help," Stake spat, seething at the idea that Santana was, in any way, responsible for what had happened to her. "We told you Gordon was out of control with power in this county, and we'd need outside help to see justice done."

Jack slammed his hat back onto his head and narrowed his eyes. "And from what I understand, part of the power Sheriff Gordon wields is a direct result of his affiliation with the Kings of Bedlam. A club you conveniently forgot to tell us you're a member of. Any lawyer will claim the Kings have a beef with Gordon and are merely trying to get rid of him."

"The Kings have nothing to do with this," Stake growled.

"So you say." Jack started to turn around but stopped mid-way. "At this point, we don't have enough evidence to charge Miss Rogers, and we probably won't continue to spend tax dollars on the case. Count yourself lucky, Miss Rogers. I know the justice system doesn't always work the way it should, but putting an innocent woman in jail isn't something I'm willing to do. Unfortunately, I don't have enough to put Gordon away." He continued, jumping off the porch to the ground below. "I wish things had turned out differently, believe me. The best thing you can do is to avoid Gordon as much as possible from here on out."

Stake watched the Rangers leave. He waited until he heard the SUV pull out of the driveway before speaking. "Gordon won't get away with it. I promise."

"I don't want you to end up like my dad," she whispered.

He swung her up into his arms and headed for the cabin. The revenge he would enact could wait while he branded Santana as his. "Are you on the pill, bug?" he asked, carrying her to his bedroom.

She shook her head.

Fuck. For the first time in his life, he wanted to empty his seed inside a woman, not any woman, his woman. "We'll take care of that tomorrow." He laid her gently on the bed and immediately pulled her shirt over her head. "Tell me you're okay with this?"

"You're the only man I've ever wanted." She unzipped her shorts and pushed them down and off.

Within seconds, she was spread out before him like a sacrificial lamb. As much as he hated the thought of another man touching her, he needed to know a few things. He pushed his jeans down, giving Santana her first glimpse of his cock. While digging a condom out of his wallet, he gave her time to look her fill, unsure of how many naked men she'd seen in the past. "Are you a virgin?"

She bit her lower lip and slowly shook her head from side to side. "I wish I was, but I was tricked into giving it to someone who only wanted *it* and not *me*."

"Who?" He tried to control his temper at the thought of someone using her. How many men would he end up killing before he defended the woman who was quickly becoming his entire world? He crawled onto the mattress and bracketed her body with his. On his hands and knees, he stared down at her, waiting for her answer.

"It doesn't matter. It was a long time ago, when I was in high school." She touched his chest before running her hands down his body. "I'm yours if you want me."

He watched as one of her delicate hands cupped his balls while the other wrapped around his dick. His body shivered at the contact, proving, once again, that her touch was different. The need to brand her, to make her his, outweighed his desire to kiss and lick every inch of her. "I need to fuck you."

She smiled for the first time since the Rangers had intruded. "I'd like that."

He moved to a kneeling position and ripped open the condom package. It felt so wrong to sheathe himself, but neither of them were ready to face the consequences of unprotected sex. He paused in the process of rolling the condom down his length. He'd always sworn he'd never settle down and have kids, but now that he had Santana, he could easily see himself settling down, even if kids still weren't an option for him.

"Stake?"

He blinked several times before continuing. Protection in place, he insinuated himself between her thighs. "Wrap yourself around me," he instructed as he guided the head of his cock to her wet pussy. He drew his crown up and down her slit several times before slowly pushing inside.

Santana pressed her palms against his chest. "Wait," she gasped, closing her eyes. "You're so much bigger than Robby was." Her eyes popped open, and she stared up at Stake, obviously realizing what she'd let slip.

"Langers?" He closed his eyes. Fucking hell, he hated that asshole.

"It doesn't matter." She moved her hands to his back, trying to pull him deeper. "I'm okay, now."

Jealousy had never played a part in his life, and the rage that threatened to overwhelm him had little to do with that damned green-eyed monster, and everything to do with the cop who'd used the woman in his arms.

"Please don't."

He opened his eyes and stared into twin kaleidoscopes. "I'm gonna kill him."

She rolled her eyes. "If you started killing everyone who treated me like shit, this place would turn into a ghost town, and you'd be sitting on death row."

Lowering himself, he sank his cock into her heated depths. Shame filled him, once again. "And I'd be at the top of the list, wouldn't I?"

Santana broke eye contact, giving him his answer. "You never treated me like shit because you forgot I was alive."

He'd give anything to go back and change the past. "I'm here now, and I'll spend the rest of my life making it up to you." He took her mouth in a deep kiss as he began to rock in and out of her pussy.

A moan escaped her as she wrapped her legs higher around his back.

"You feel so good," he whispered against her lips as his hips snapped, creating a staccato beat as their flesh slapped together. "I want you on the pill so I can fuck you whenever and wherever I want."

"You can already do that," she panted in his ear.

He gave her a quick kiss. "Not yet, but soon." He reached down and centered her clit between his thumb and forefinger. Pinching the sensitive nub, he nearly lost it when she bucked under him. "Yeah, move for me," he urged.

With a soft groan, she locked her legs around him and started to move under him, meeting each of his thrusts. Fuck, it was a beautiful feeling to be with someone who actually meant something to him. He sought her mouth with his own in another dance of tongues. Christ, had he ever enjoyed kissing so much? Usually fucking was a way to relieve stress and the bullshit of the day, but everything felt different with Santana. He'd worried that his attraction had more to do with her need for protection, but as he buried his cock time after time, he realized protection had nothing to do with the way she made him feel.

"Stake!" she cried while her body shook with the force of her climax.

"So fucking beautiful," he groaned as he pumped inside her twice more before burying himself deep. He shot into the condom, wishing again that the fucking thing wasn't between them. *Soon*, he told himself as he collapsed on top of her.

He rolled to her side and removed the condom. "I need to talk to the club, and I'm gonna need you to come with me."

She shook her head. "I can't go there."

"Yes, you can." As much as he wanted to make love to her all night long, there were things that needed doing. With Gordon free, it was only a matter of time before the sonofabitch tried to get at her again. "I need to meet with my brothers because it's important they agree that you're under the club's protection from now on."

He didn't want to worry her, but he needed to be honest. "Gordon's days are numbered, and I need them to accept that."

She snuggled against him and rested her cheek on his chest. "You have a great body." She traced the words tattooed sideways up his torso. "The road is eternal, the wind constant," she read. "That's beautiful. Did you come up with that?"

Stake shook his head. "I read it somewhere, but it always stuck with me. It's the reason I ride. It's a feeling of freedom that I can't explain to people who don't own a bike."

He cupped her left breast. "But, enough of my body. I'm torn between wanting to never see you wear a bra again or asking you to put one on to hide these gorgeous tits from the brothers at the club."

"I don't want anyone but you," she said. "But I've seen your collection of magazines, so I know you're rather fond of tits."

Fuck, and didn't that make him feel like the luckiest man on earth. "Most of 'em in those magazines are fake. I hate fake tits." He rolled onto his side and scooted down to suck one of her nipples into his mouth. "Yours are fuckin' perfect."

"No bra it is then," she replied with a giggle.

The sound was so unexpected it caught him off guard. He released her nipple. "That's the first time I think I've heard you laugh since..."

She shrugged. "I feel good."

"I hope to make you feel really good later after we get back from the club." He gave her a quick kiss. "Making you feel good has become my new favorite pastime."

Chapter Five

Wearing a pair of denim shorts and a tight red tank top, Santana climbed onto the back of Stake's Harley. It would be the first time since her dad was sent to prison that she'd been on a bike, and knowing she was on Stake's bike made it so much better. She settled as close as she could get and rested her hands on his muscular abdomen.

He shook his head and moved her hands to rest on his cock. "This is where I want your hands whenever you're with me," he said over his shoulder before starting the bike.

She pressed her cheek against the soft leather of his cut and held onto his groin as he rode out of the driveway. She'd remembered to pile her hair on top of her head before putting on the half-helmet and as the wind whipped across her face, she was grateful for it.

Freedom. She recalled Stake using that word earlier when he'd talked about riding. He was so right. As they wound their way over the ribbon of county roads in the darkness, she felt like a different person. All the worry of being left behind by him vanished, replaced by the kind of hope she'd never allowed herself. One thing she was sure of, she would take care of Gordon herself. Stake had already given her more than anyone ever had, and she refused to use that connection to rid the world of an asshole like the sheriff. If she screwed up and went to prison, at least she'd known what kindness really felt like.

* * * *

Stake parked in his usual spot and helped Santana off the bike. Before releasing her, he unbuttoned her shorts and shoved his hand down the front to her pussy. He slid his fingers up and down the wet slit. "You're so fucking wet. I knew you were my kind of woman." He sank two fingers inside her pussy and gathered some of her cream before removing them. Holding her gaze, he tasted her sweet juices and shook his head. "I'm a lucky bastard."

She lowered her chin, breaking eye contact. "I'm the lucky one," she whispered.

The club door opened and light spilled out into the parking lot. He buttoned her shorts before wrapping an arm around her waist. "You ready for this?"

She shrugged.

"Stay close until I have to speak with Cecil. When that happens, I'll find someone I trust to keep an eye on you, and whatever you do, don't take shit from any of the club bitches," he warned.

"Have you slept with a lot of them?" she asked.

He stopped walking and turned her to face him. "What I have or haven't done with any cunt in that building has nothing to do with you. Got it?" He started to leave it at that, but decided to go a step further. "I told you, you're mine, and I'm yours. That's something no one else can ever claim."

She licked her lips. "I'm nervous."

"That's good, because some of my brothers don't know fuck all about how to treat a lady. That's why you need to stick close until I have time to school the bastards." He pressed his lips against hers and thrust his tongue inside before pulling back. He grinned and shook his head. He didn't have a clue as to how one little thing could bring him so easily to his knees.

He opened the door of the club and ushered her inside, keeping a tight hold on her hand. He nodded to his brothers as he wove through the tables to the bar. "Beer?" he asked her.

He could tell that by the way she contemplated the question that the offer worried her. He leaned down and whispered in her ear. "It's a beer. Don't worry, I won't let you drink too much."

"I don't ever want to be like my momma."

"I know," he soothed, kissing her temple. "Two beers," he told Mad Dog.

Mad Dog's gaze landed on Santana. "Fuck, Stake, who's this?"

"Mine," Stake answered, pulling Santana against him. "And you'd better watch yourself, or I'll tell Corrine."

Santana glanced up at the skinny man. "Santana Rogers," she said, introducing herself.

Mad Dog glanced at Stake.

"Yeah, this is Smash's daughter." If he was going to have trouble with anyone because of Ellie's relationship to Santana, he needed to put an end to it fast.

Mad Dog smiled. "Nice to meet you. I didn't know your dad, but everyone speaks highly of him."

It was Santana's turn to give Stake a questioning glance. He gave her a reassuring squeeze. "I told you, bug, it was Ellie, not Smash."

She nodded and accepted the bottle of beer. "Thank you," she told Mad Dog.

Mad Dog winked. "Anytime, sweetie."

Stake leaned across the bar. "To you, her name's Santana, not sweetie, babe, or hon. Got that?"

Mad Dog nodded but had enough sense not to answer.

Satisfied that Mad Dog would treat Santana with the respect she deserved, Stake studied the room, looking for a place to sit. That goddamned Iggy was getting a blow job right next to the chair Stake usually sat in and he wouldn't subject Santana to that. Iggy was a fucking pig, and his lack of discretion was really getting on Stake's nerves. He pointed to a couch in the sitting area of the club. There were several brothers with bitches on their laps, but they appeared to be behaving themselves for the time being. "Let's sit over there."

Santana grabbed his arm. "Oh my God, is that Tiny?"

He nodded, knowing the two of them went to school together. "You used to be friends, right?"

Her expression fell. "Used to be." She pointed to a table in front of the door. "What's wrong with that one?"

"It's not safe to sit in front of the door. Too easy for someone to walk through and level their gun on the first person they see," he replied.

"It's safer for me because it would put me closer to an escape," she mumbled.

Laughing, Tiny met Stake's gaze. He glanced at Santana and the blood seemed to drain from his face as he got to his feet. "Too late, Tiny's spotted you."

"I need to go to the bathroom." Santana started to pull away, but Stake kept his arm firmly around her.

"No, you need to stand up for yourself. Whatever happened between the two of you, you need to understand that it wasn't his fault."

Tears sprang to her eyes as she stared up at Stake. "I can't."

"Santana," Tiny said, approaching them.

Santana refused to look at the burly young biker. "Hi, Tiny," she replied, her face pressed against Stake's chest.

"Ummm, I was sorry to hear about what happened," Tiny said, obviously as uncomfortable as Santana.

Part of Stake wanted to shake her for the way she was acting, but a bigger part understood. She'd been alone for years, and although he was grateful she'd accepted him so easily back into her life, he couldn't fault her for being wary of everyone else who'd hurt her. "Give us a minute," he told Tiny before leading Santana to the opposite side of the room. He guided her down a hallway to the back door of the club.

Once in the warm night air, he led her to a grouping of picnic tables they used for family cookouts. He sat on one of the benches and pulled her between his thighs, pressing his cheek against her tits.

"I'm sorry," she said, running her fingers through his hair.

"You need to understand that no one here wanted to turn their backs on you. The club was put in a no-win situation by Ellie, and we did what we had to do. I know you've been hurt, and I wish like hell I could take it away, but I can't, and unless you learn to forgive these people, you'll never fit in." He nuzzled his face against her breasts. "I need you to fit in, because I don't plan on ever giving you up, and these people are my family."

Santana put her hands on his cheeks and tilted his head back to look up at her. "I'll try to be nice, but I don't think I'll ever be able to trust that they won't leave me alone again."

"Do you feel that way about me, too?" he asked.

She nodded. "There's no one I want to be with more, but I know it could all end tomorrow. You're a biker, and I know how easy it is for you to get women. You're with me because I'm different, but that won't last long. Someday, you'll see me just as you see the others."

Stake removed her hands from his face and brought them to his mouth. He reverently kissed each finger, trying like hell to convey his promise. She was it for him, and he knew that in his soul, but he doubted she would believe him because why should she? He didn't have the best track record where Santana was concerned. "Guess I'll just have to prove you wrong about that."

* * * *

"I need to talk to Cecil," Stake said. "It might be a good time for you to talk to Tiny."

Santana took a sip of her beer. The last thing she wanted was to go back into the clubhouse, but Stake was right. She needed to get the talk with Tiny over with. "Can you send him out here? I'd feel better without people watching us."

Stake pushed his hand under her shirt and caressed her pebbled nipple as he stared up at her. "I can't leave you out here by yourself."

"Despite everything he's done, I know Tiny won't hurt me." Although Tiny hadn't spoken to her, she had a feeling he was the one who'd given Robby Langers the black eye and split lip after Robby started bragging about popping her cherry.

Stake pulled his phone out and punched in some numbers before putting it to his ear. "Hey, grab Santana a fresh beer, and come out to the picnic tables." He nodded. "Yeah," he said before hanging up. "He's gonna hit the head first."

She couldn't help but laugh. "Do you have any idea how many times I've seen that boy pee against the side of a tree?"

Stake pinched her nipple. "He's smarter than that now. He knows I'd cut his fucking dick off if he whipped it out in front of you again."

Each time he showed his alpha streak, it made her pussy clench. "Yes, sir." She moved to sit on his lap. Resting her head on his shoulder, she buried her face in his neck. "Call Tiny back and tell him we're going to fuck before you talk to Cecil."

He squeezed her ass. "I won't disrespect you like that. You deserve more than to be fucked a few steps away from a bunch of drunk bikers."

Even though she wasn't going to get what she craved, her heart warmed at his answer. "Okay," she whispered as she heard the door shut. She leaned in and gave him a deep kiss. "Please don't be gone long."

"Just long enough. Promise." He stood with her still in his arms and set her on top of the picnic table. "Watch her," he told Tiny. "Anyone tries to mess with her, shoot 'em."

Tiny chuckled and handed Santana a beer. "Will do."

Stake smiled at her once more before turning to head inside.

"Mind if I sit?" Tiny asked.

She gestured to the other end of the table. "Help yourself." She took a sip of her fresh, cold beer and sighed. She really did enjoy the taste, even if she was afraid to like it too much.

"I'm sorry I hurt you," Tiny said. For a man of six-seven that had to weigh at least two hundred and fifty pounds, all of it solid muscle, he sounded like the little boy she'd first met when she was five years old. "I'll make it up to you."

She fought hard to remember the position her mom had put everyone in. Stake was right, it wasn't Tiny's fault, but that didn't erase the years of pain and loneliness. "I don't know what to say."

Tiny tugged on his beard. "You don't have to say anything. I'm the one who fucked up. I should've been strong enough to go against my dad and the club."

"No." She scooted over enough to reach Tiny's big hand. "I don't think I'll ever be the girl I used to be, but now I know it was my mom's fault. Doesn't make it any easier to stomach, and I'll probably never feel comfortable around the club, but that doesn't mean I don't understand why it happened."

Tiny sandwiched her hand between both of his. "Will you tell me what's going on with Stake? I take it the two of you are finally together."

She took a deep breath. God, she needed someone to talk to other than Stake, but trusting Tiny after everything that had happened scared her. "I've always loved Stake, you know that."

Tiny smiled. "I think everyone knew that except Stake."

"Gordon's going to get away with what he did," she announced. "Stake's talking to Cecil about it."

"Stake'll kill Gordon," Tiny realized.

"Yeah, but I can't let him do that." She squeezed Tiny's arm with her free hand. "I can't let him go to prison because of me."

Tiny shook his head. "He won't let it go. That isn't who he is."

She wanted to tell Tiny that she planned to deal with Gordon on her own, but she wouldn't make Tiny an accessory. She decided to change the subject. "Do you still talk to Jaycee and Gill?"

He released her hand and reached back for his beer. "They got married, if you can believe that shit."

Stunned, she reached for her own beer. She suddenly felt as if she was back in high school. "Oh my God, how'd that happen?"

"Wouldn't I like to know." He slapped his knee. "I never told Gill this, but I always thought he was gay. He never dated. All he wanted to do was hang out with me and Jaycee." He started to laugh, the sound so deep Santana felt it in her chest. "I'm happy for them, ya know, but now they're living in Oregon, and I'm here."

Santana finally felt comfortable enough to reach out and tug on Tiny's long beard. "If you'd shave this, I bet you'd find someone special."

"Are you kidding? This thing's a pussy magnet."

She rolled her eyes. "I'll have to take your word for it."

* * * *

Stake knocked on Cecil's door. "Got a minute?"

"Come in." Cecil was sitting at his desk, talking to Magic and Hog. "Good. We were just discussing you."

Stake tried to figure out why the fuck they'd been discussing him. He doubted Cecil knew about Gordon unless the sheriff had already called. "What's up?"

"Penny told Hog you had an issue with the drugs." Cecil narrowed his eyes. "Is this going to become a problem?"

Oddly enough, with everything else going on, he hadn't given a lot of thought to the hard drugs he'd seen in the club's San Antonio headquarters. "Not unless you expect me to deal 'em, but if I'm going to keep working with the girls, I want them cut off that shit. Penny looks thinner and older than the last time I saw her. It's just common sense to take care of our assets."

"When the girls use, we make more because they do it with their johns," Hog argued.

Stake hooked his thumbs in his front pockets. "Then put me on protection."

"You're good with the whores," Cecil said.

"I'm good with drug-free whores. Seriously, Prez, I don't have the stomach for it after what went down with Smash." He looked pointedly at Cecil, letting the prez know he knew what had really gone down the day Smash had shot the cop. It had been Cecil's reckless driving that had caught the attention of the patrolman. With the car loaded with drugs, Cecil had panicked and reached for his gun. When the young officer had taken aim and fired a wayward shot at Cecil with his own gun, Smash had shot the cop from the passenger side of the car, saving Cecil's life. "You want the drug business, fine, but I want nothing to do with it."

"You're part of this club," Hog reminded Stake. "You do what we say."

"No," Stake disagreed. "I follow the majority vote, and unless there was a meeting I wasn't informed of, there was no vote on meth and heroin."

Hog got to his feet to face off with Stake. "You disrespectful sonofabitch."

Stake glanced at Cecil. "Call off your guard dog before I put the old man in the ground." At close to sixty-five, Hog talked a big game, but he was no match for Stake's speed and strength.

"You fuckin' punk," Hog said, charging toward Stake.

Stake stepped to the side and connected a hard punch to Hog's ribs. "Cecil."

"That's enough," Cecil finally announced, getting to his feet to come around from behind the desk. He walked up to Stake and stared him in the eyes. "Don't push me."

"Or what?" Stake was tired of the bullshit. Most of the newly patched club members had no respect, and the old dogs were so fucking full of themselves that they thought they could start making up their own rules. Well, Stake hadn't signed up for that, and he'd be damned if he'd stick around if that's the way things were going to be. "Maybe when I take Santana to the Barbeque and Blues run in Fayetteville in October, I should just stay " The Kings had several chapters sprinkled around the southern half of the United States. Maybe getting her away from Gordon and Broken Ridge would be the best thing for them.

"Don't start that shit," Cecil growled.

It wasn't the first time Stake had asked for a transfer to another chapter. Soon after Smash had been killed, he hadn't been able to stand to look at his uncle and had practically begged to be let loose to go somewhere else. At the time, Cecil had refused, telling Stake it would kill his mother if he moved away. Stake knew it was bullshit. The only time his mom even remembered she had a son was when she was between husbands or boyfriends and needed something fixed.

"Gordon got off. He's gonna walk away with only a few stitches," Stake announced, keeping one eye on Cecil and the other on Hog, who was rubbing his side. "The way I see it, either Gordon needs to fucking die, or I need to get Santana the hell away from this town." He planned to take care of Gordon regardless, but Cecil didn't need to know that.

"The cops'll expect you to act on Gordon, so you'd best lay your ass low for the time being," Cecil ordered, leaning back to sit on the edge of his desk. "You continue to make weekly trips to check on the girls and stop giving them shit about the drugs, and I'll think about a transfer between now and the Fayetteville ride."

"Who's going to watch Santana when I'm gone? If you think I'm leaving her alone with someone like Gordon running loose, you're fucking crazy." No way would Stake take Santana to check in on a bunch of whores. She might be aware that the Kings peddled pussy, but that didn't mean he wanted her around it.

"We'll figure something out," Cecil replied.

"What's going on between the two of you?" Magic asked.

"She's mine, and that's all you need to know." Stake wondered if the VP's question had anything to do with his daughter.

"She your old lady then?" Cecil asked.

Although he hadn't discussed that sort of arrangement with Santana, Stake felt confident in his feelings. "Looks that way. Which means the Kings are done paying Gordon."

"Easier said than done," Hog said.

"What if Gordon tried to rape Alma? Would you still work with him?" Stake asked.

Hog made a face. "Hell, if Gordon could pry Alma's legs apart, he'd be doing better than me."

Stake took a step toward the Sergeant at Arms. "It's not a fuckin' joke, asshole!"

"We can't just stop paying him. Gordon knows our schedules," Cecil argued.

Stake couldn't believe what he'd just heard. "I thought you were all about protecting innocents."

Cecil held up his hand. "Don't take this the wrong way, but I can't throw away our relationship with Gordon because of the fucked up situation with Santana."

In that moment, Stake knew he was leaving Broken Ridge, with or without Cecil's permission. He loved being part of a brotherhood, but the Broken Ridge chapter no longer felt like home. "One month," he said, holding up a finger as he turned and left the office.

* * * *

By the time Stake walked out of the clubhouse, Santana and Tiny had managed to get somewhat reacquainted. She doubted their friendship would ever fully recover, but she was confident that she could talk to Tiny if she needed to.

"Hey," she greeted Stake with a kiss. Although he kissed her back, she could tell something was wrong. "How'd it go?"

"Not good." He glanced at Tiny. "Thanks for keeping an eye on my girl."

Tiny slid off the table. "No problem." He slapped Stake on the back. "Catch up with you two later."

As soon as Tiny disappeared into the club, Stake sat down and pulled her onto his lap. "There's a big gathering in Fayetteville, Arkansas in October. I want you to go with me."

"Okay," she agreed. "I've always wanted to go with you on a run."

He kissed her temple. "Something's been bothering me, and I keep telling myself to give you more time, but I think it's time we talked."

"What's wrong?" She bit her bottom lip. Had Cecil told Stake to get rid of her? She wouldn't put it past that creepy bastard.

He sighed. "I need to know about the drawings and the shirt." He tipped her chin up. "I know you had a crush on me when you were younger, but was it more than that?"

Embarrassed by the question, she broke eye contact. "You're the only man I've ever wanted, but until a few days ago, you couldn't see me as a woman."

"That's not true." He maneuvered her until she straddled his lap, putting the bulge in his jeans against her pussy. "I saw you about seven years ago."

She nodded, remembering how badly it had hurt when he'd stopped to talk to Gordon and hadn't even bothered to come over and say hi to her. "I was sunbathing."

"Yeah, and your tits were so fucking unbelievable that I got hard on the spot," he confessed.

"So why didn't you make a move then? Why now?" She'd been almost eighteen with a mother who hadn't even noticed she was alive. Even though a part of her had hated him, she still would have welcomed his attention.

"You weren't legal, and even dead, Smash was still my best friend."

"I never understood why you liked my dad. He was such a bastard."

"Smash was loyal to me, your mother, and the club. To you, yeah, he was a real sonofabitch for a while. I can't tell you how many times I asked him why he was so hard on you, and he could never give me an answer."

"Do you think he hated me?" It was a question she'd asked herself so many times. She'd never understood why he got so mad at her every time he drank. How he could hit his own flesh and blood?

"No." He cupped her face in his hands. Tears filled his eyes, surprising the hell out of her. "I think…" He shook his head and cleared his throat. "I think he noticed you as a woman, and it filled him with so much shame that he took that anger out on you."

The thought disgusted her, but something niggled in the back of her mind. In her early years, Smash had been somewhat kind to her. It wasn't until after she'd started her menstrual cycle that he seemed to change the way he treated her. She couldn't believe she'd never made the connection. Her hand flew to her mouth as she scrambled off Stake's lap. "I think I'm gonna be sick."

Stake was at her side in no time, wrapping an arm around her waist to steady her as he tried to hold her hair back. Her body lurched as she lost her battle to hold it in. Thoughts of her father watching her when she hadn't been aware spiraled through her head. Had she ever changed in front of him? Had he ever snuck into the bathroom while she'd taken a shower? Another round of vomit splashed to the ground as she started to cry. She'd always known her mom didn't love her, but to find out her dad might have loved her so much he felt the need to beat her every time he got drunk and felt guilty was so fucking sick.

Stake wiped her mouth with the black bandana he usually kept folded in his back pocket. "It's okay, lady bug. I've got you." He swung her up into his arms and took off around the building to the parking lot.

She clung to Stake. "I know I should be grateful that he didn't do anything beyond beating me, but I hate him more than I ever have."

He set her on the back of his bike. "Are you well enough to hang on?" he asked as he buckled her helmet's chinstrap.

"Yeah, I'm okay. Just take me home. I need a shower." She wasn't okay. The revelation about her father did more to screw her up than Gordon could have ever hoped to. Gordon was a pig, but her dad…

Stake climbed on the bike and directed her hands on his stomach instead of his cock. "Just for tonight."

She closed her eyes and leaned against him as they took off.

* * * *

Once they arrived at the house, Stake gave Santana time alone in the bathroom. When he heard sobs through the bathroom door, it took all his strength not to barge in and wrap her in his arms.

He hadn't known if his suspicions of Smash were right, but it was damn obvious Santana did. "Fuck." He dragged his fingers through his hair as he paced the bedroom floor. As sick as it was, he gave his friend credit for not acting on his desires. As much as the beatings had affected Santana, rape would have destroyed her.

The door opened and she came out wearing nothing but a goddamn towel. He clenched his hands into fists in an effort to control himself. In her present state, whatever happened between them needed to be initiated by her.

"I know you said you noticed my body that day when I was sunbathing, but did you ever see me as woman before that?" she asked, her voice still thick from the tears she'd shed.

Holy fucking Christ, how could he answer that question? Had he noticed she was growing into a gorgeous woman, hell yes. If he told her the truth, would she turn away from him? He stared at her for a long time before answering. "Yeah," he whispered. "I definitely noticed the changes in you as you grew older."

Her dark eyebrows drew together as she bit her bottom lip. He could tell it wasn't the answer she'd wanted. He took several steps toward the door. Her apparent disgust was fucking killing him. "I'll understand if you want to sleep in your room."

It was the best he could do. He hadn't even told her the whole truth and he'd hurt her. "I'm sorry."

Santana dropped her towel and casually walked over to the bed. Rumpled from their earlier lovemaking, the bed looked huge as she slid onto the mattress.

"Santana?" he asked as she pulled a sheet over her naked body.

She rolled to her side, away from him, and sighed. "I wish you would've loved me enough to take me away from them."

He knew she was referring to Ellie and Smash. The statement broke his heart. He quickly undressed and joined her in bed, spooning against her back. "Had I taken you away with me, I would've been no different than your dad," he confessed. He buried his face in her thick hair. "There's a light in you that seems to shine only for me. It's always been that way. When you were a kid, every time I'd go on the road and see something amazing, I wished you were there with me to experience it, too. I told myself it was because you were the only person who seemed happy to see me, and maybe it was." He shook his head. "All I know is that I've loved you in one form or another since I met you."

He blew out a ragged breath. The depth of what he'd just admitted cut him to the bone. "Once you were older, I got as close as I dared. Believe me, I thought of taking you away more than once, but I knew how you felt about me and in my heart, I knew I wouldn't have been able to push you away."

She reached for his hand and put it on her breast. "I'm not a little girl anymore."

He felt her nipple harden against his palm. "No, you're not." Which is why he was going to take her away from the people who still possessed the power to hurt her. "I have to make a few trips into San Antonio over the next month to check on the girls."

"The prostitutes?" she asked, her body going rigid.

"Yeah, but it's tying up some loose ends for the club." He gave her tit a gentle squeeze. "It's club business, bug, it's part of a deal I'm trying to work out with Cecil."

"Do you fuck them?"

He moved enough to force her back to the mattress. "I've never fucked them." He leaned down and took her nipple into his mouth. He sucked and licked the pebbled nub for several moments before releasing her. "I think that's why the girls trust me so much." He teased the nipple with the tip of his tongue. "I told you earlier, I'm yours. I've never said that to anyone, so you can believe I don't take it lightly."

"Can I go with you?"

He shook his head. "I can ask Tiny to stay with you while I'm gone. That is, if the two of you have worked through your differences?"

"We have." She ran her fingers over his chin. "I like the stubble, but promise you won't grow a beard again."

He chuckled, knowing Tiny's bushy beard had prompted the request. "You've made your opinion of beards quite clear, and I haven't grown one since you told me that first time." He grinned and threw the sheet back before moving to insinuate himself between her legs. "But…" He stared at her pink pussy and groaned. "You need to understand that a beard is softer than stubble when I'm eating your pussy."

She gasped as he pressed his mouth against her cunt.

Chapter Six

Dressed in one of Stake's T-shirts, Santana slid bacon and scrambled eggs onto two plates as Stake entered the kitchen. "Morning."

He sandwiched her between him and the counter as he filled a mug with coffee. "Still sore?" he asked, grinding his erection against her.

She was, but not enough to pass up morning sex. "A little."

He narrowed his eyes as he took a sip of coffee. "Liar." He stepped back and sat in his chair.

It was then that she noticed the wet washcloth and bottle of lube. Was he planning to fuck her? Between the whisker burn and hours of fucking, she wasn't sure she could handle it, despite her body wanting nothing more than to feel him again. She set the plates on the table, and he promptly pulled her plate in front of his chair alongside his. He patted his lap. "Come here, bug."

"Okay, yes, I lied. I'm sore," she confessed.

He simply nodded and gestured to his lap again. "Sit," he ordered.

With trepidation, she did as instructed, wincing when her bare ass brushed against the denim of his jeans. She blushed as she remembered him licking not only her pussy but her asshole, as well. It was mortifying to think about in the light of day, but she hadn't been able to tell him no. The attention to her ass had been unbelievable even though it wasn't something she'd ever considered doing with a partner.

Stake pushed her legs apart and picked up the wet washcloth. "Relax," he whispered in her ear as he pressed the cold cloth against her sore cunt. "Those eggs look good."

She picked up the fork and speared several of the fluffy yellow mounds before holding it to his lips. "Is that your subtle way of asking me to feed you?"

He ran his free hand up under her shirt to squeeze her breast. "My hands are full."

She leaned against his chest as she followed the eggs with a slice of bacon. The cool cloth on her pussy felt fantastic, but his attention to her tits was making her wet. "I could get used to this."

"I'm counting on it." He removed the cloth from her raw skin and fit it under her ass before reaching for the lube. "This'll help, too." He poured lube onto his fingers as she continued to feed him. "You should be fine tonight, but keep applying lube to the chafed areas today." He smeared the lube on the outside of her pussy lips before separating them to take care of her most intimate parts. When he zeroed in on her clit, her entire body jerked.

"Oh, fuck," she panted, dropping the fork onto the table.

With another deep chuckle, he continued to pluck and rub her clit as her body bucked against him. "Push the dishes to the other side of the table."

She looked up at him. "What're you going to do?"

"Your delicate pussy isn't the only thing that's sore, is it?" he asked.

Fuck. Fuck. Fuck. He was going to touch her ass again. She didn't move right away, and he scowled. "I thought you enjoyed what I did last night?"

"I did, but we were in bed, and the lights were off." She cursed herself for acting like such a virgin. She had no doubt Stake had done a number of things with other women. Most of which she would probably find shocking, and she knew if she didn't do everything to keep him satisfied, he'd go elsewhere. As she pushed away the plates, she reminded herself that she had liked the feel of his tongue on her asshole. She simply needed to get over her embarrassment and let loose with him. "Okay."

"Take off your T-shirt, and lay on your back," he ordered, lifting her onto the table to face him.

When she pulled the shirt over her head, the loose knot she'd tied her hair in to cook fell out, leaving it to tumble down.

"Goddamn," he growled. "You're so fucking beautiful." His gaze traveled from her face to her tits before roaming south to her pussy. He shook his head. "I don't deserve you."

The statement surprised her, but made her more determined than ever to give him what he wanted. The more she gave of herself, the hornier he seemed to get. She decided to put her fears and embarrassment aside and embrace the sexual woman inside her that had waited too long to be with the man she loved. Lying back on the table, she rested her feet on the edge. With a grin, she spread her legs wide open, giving him a view of what his five o'clock shadow had done to her.

"Oh, babe." He leaned in and licked her pussy, despite the lube he'd already used on her.

She was thankful he had taken the time to shave before setting down for breakfast. He drew back and reached for the lube. "I'm dying to fuck you, but I won't let myself."

For that, she was only slightly grateful. "Later?" she asked, praying she'd never again have to go a night without his cock. She really was turning into a slut, but she supposed it didn't really count if it was with Stake.

He dripped cold lube onto her chafed skin and rubbed it around with a light touch. "Is this okay?"

"Mmm hmm," she answered, unable to form words while she squirmed with pleasure. She reached for her tits and began squeezing her hardened nipples.

When Stake's lubed fingers circled her asshole, she gasped. "Someday, I'd like to try fucking you here." He pressed the tip of his thumb against her puckered opening until it popped inside.

"Oh," she gasped again as he pushed farther into her.

With his thumb buried inside her ass, he used tip of his middle finger to manipulate her clit. The combination skyrocketed her into a climax, stealing her breath. She fought for air as the orgasm ripped through her.

Stake noticed her distress and gathered her in his arms. "Babe. Breathe," he soothed, peppering her face with kisses. He pulled her off the table and cradled her on his lap. "It's okay."

Although her body continued to experience small quakes, her breathing slowly returned to normal. "What the hell was that?" she panted.

"Evidently, a damn good orgasm." He kissed her forehead. "You scared the shit outta me."

She nodded and opened her eyes. "Wow."

* * * *

Two days later, Stake found Santana sitting on the back porch swing he'd put up for her the previous evening. He handed her a beer and sat beside her. "I have to go to San Antonio on Thursday, but I thought you might want to take the trip to the cemetery tomorrow. If we leave early enough, we should be there and back before dark."

She took a sip of her beer. "I don't think I'm ready to go to the cemetery." She lifted his arm and draped it over her as she snuggled against his side. "I may never be ready."

"What about your mom's ashes?" He understood that she was still processing the realization that her own father had been attracted to her, but he wanted her to have the closure with Ellie that he felt she needed.

She buried her face against his chest. "Is it wrong that I don't care about what happens to them? I keep thinking about how miserable she made my life, and a part of me wants to defy her wishes in death." She looked up at Stake. "I've never been to Dad's grave, and I don't think I'm ready. When he killed that cop, he killed my future, not that he gave a shit because the club always came first." Her eyes drifted shut as she hugged Stake. "For the first time in my life, I don't want to worry what either of them would think of my actions. I'm doing this for me, because it's what I need right now."

He wanted to tell her about Cecil's involvement in the shooting, but club business was just that, and telling her the truth would only put her in jeopardy. He kissed the top of her head. "When you're ready, just let me know."

She nodded but didn't look at him or speak.

Their peaceful moment was interrupted by the sound of a car in the driveway. "I swear I'm going to put up a damn security gate," he mumbled.

Santana's body went rigid. "Do you think they're here for me?"

He gave her a deep kiss before getting to his feet. "Stay here, and I'll get rid of whoever it is." He jumped off the porch and walked around to the side of the cabin. As soon as he saw the cherry red Crossfire, he groaned.

When he saw no sign of Rachel, he stalked to the front of the house. There she was in all her bleached and silicone glory. "What're you doing here?" he asked before she could knock on the front door.

Rachel spun around to face him. "Dad told me you have that Rogers slut living here. I came by to see if it was true." She came toward him with fire in her bright blue eyes.

He held up his hand. "Get off my property," he warned, so pissed he wanted to wrap his hands around her neck and squeeze. "And if I ever hear you refer to Santana that way again, I'll forget you're a woman."

Crossing her arms, Rachel purposely tried to display her big, fake tits to their best advantage. "Everyone's talking about how you've gone crazy over that bitch. How do you think that makes me feel?"

Stake tilted his head from side to side, popping his neck, in an attempt to control his anger. Unfortunately, it didn't work. He grabbed her by the upper arm in a bruising grip and jerked her toward her car as he walked. Santana had suffered years of verbal abuse from people like Rachel, and he be goddamned if he'd let her taint the home he was trying to build with Santana. He opened the door with such force he was surprised the metal didn't buckle, but he wouldn't have given a shit if it had. He caught Santana out of the corner of his eye and knew she was watching and probably wondering who Rachel was.

Before shoving Rachel back in her car, he leaned in until they were nose to nose so only she could hear him. "If you ever bring your skank ass to my home again, I'll fucking kill you. And if I ever hear you talking about Santana, I'll tell the whole club that your pussy's rancid shit, and they should stay away." He grinned at the disbelieving expression on her face. "Yeah, even your father. I think he deserves to know just what a whore his perfect little princess is."

"I'm not afraid of you," she shot back.

With his hands braced on the roof of the car, he leaned down. "You should be, but in case you really believe I won't lay a hand on you because you're a woman, maybe I'll give Santana back her knife and tell her what you said about her."

Rachel's face went pale. Before she could spout more venom, he stepped back and slammed her door shut. He stood there until she peeled out of his drive before turning to face Santana. "I'm sorry about that."

Without a word, she turned and disappeared around the back of the house.

"Shit." With a sigh, he went after her. He jumped onto the porch to find she'd resumed her seat on the swing. He wasn't good at apologies, but he knew he owed her one, so he dropped down beside her. "That was Rachel, Magic's daughter," he began.

"Yeah. I remember her. I'm assuming she's one of your girlfriends?"

"No." He stretched his arm across the back of the swing and buried his fingers in her hair. "I fucked her a couple of times, but that's all it was. I told her that at the time and a couple since. Had I known she was a batshit crazy bitch, I'd have never done it the first place." He slid his hand down to Santana's shoulder and pulled her closer. "I'm sorry she came here, but she won't be back." He knew he needed to prepare her for future run-ins, though. "If she ever tries to give you a hard time, you need to take that bitch down. It's the only way you'll earn the respect of the other old ladies."

"I'm used to being on the receiving end of pain, so I'm not sure I could intentionally hurt someone." Her breath caught with a tiny gasp. "I hurt Gordon." She covered her mouth with her hand. "Oh my God, I just realized that."

He tilted her chin up. "Don't. Gordon deserved everything he got and more. Do not blame yourself."

She shook her head. "I don't. It's just hard to believe that I fought back for the first time in my life." Tears filled her eyes. "I've been worried that something was wrong with me because I didn't feel bad about what happened to me, but I think I just realized that I didn't see myself as a victim because I fought back," she said, drawing the last three words out.

"Fuck." He ran his fingers through his hair in an attempt to get it off his face. He'd thought only of the attack on her, not what she'd done to protect herself. "You're right," he agreed.

"I need you to teach me how to shoot a gun," she proclaimed, squaring her shoulders.

There was something in the tone of her voice that bothered him...resolve maybe? "I'll teach you, but are we talking self-defense, or are you going to go on some sort of rampage against everyone who's ever hurt you?"

Santana bit her bottom lip. "There's only one person I plan to get even with."

"No!" he growled. "I told you, I'll take care of Gordon. As soon as the heat dies down a bit, he'll get what's coming to him."

She straddled his lap and faced him. "And if you get caught?" Tears filled her eyes. "You've shown me more kindness in a week than I've ever known. Losing you isn't something I can survive."

He grabbed her ass and pulled her closer, smashing his mouth against hers. He put all the love he had into the kiss, trying like hell to convey with actions how deeply his feelings went. For the first time in his life, he felt loved, and he would do anything for her. How could he make her understand?

He broke the kiss, and rested his forehead on her shoulder. Fuck, he wished he was good with words. Maybe if he shared a piece of himself, she would realize that she was the only woman who could break down his defenses. It wouldn't be enough, he knew that, but it was a start. "You know that biker names are given, right?"

"Yeah, well, I know Dad got his because he was a petty smash and grab hoodlum in his younger days."

"Do you know where I got mine?" he asked. He'd never told anyone the story he was about to share with her.

"No." She ran her fingers through his hair, knowing the action always soothed him.

"My name's Jakob, but ever since I could remember, my mom's called me Stake. I thought it was cool when I started school because I was the only kid in kindergarten with a biker name." He took a breath, needing a moment to compose himself. "When I was in the fifth grade, we had to draw a family tree, but I had no idea who my father was. I went home after school, and my mom was drinking. I think her newest boyfriend was there, but I don't remember who he was."

He shook his head. "Doesn't matter. They never stayed, anyway. So, I start asking my mom questions because my project was due the next day. She told me she didn't know who my father was, and that I was a drunken *mistake* that should've never happened, which is where my nickname came from." It took everything he had to breathe after admitting to the woman he loved that his own mom still considered him a mistake.

"I'll never call you Stake again," she whispered into his ear. She'd always hated Stake's mom, but now she had even more reason to detest the woman. "I guess I never paid attention to the way it was spelled because I always thought it was the brothers teasing you because the ladies thought you were a hot piece of meat." She hugged him tight. "Which, by the way, I've always agreed with."

He looked up at Santana and couldn't help but chuckle through his pain. Fuck. "Jakob's a name that I don't identify with, but I like the thought of you calling me your big, juicy piece of meat."

"Hot piece of meat," she corrected with a slight grin on her gorgeous face.

"Anyway, the reason I told you is because I need you to understand that I feel about you the same way you feel about me. You're the first person I've ever let in, and the thought of you going anywhere near Gordon again makes me sick to my stomach. I'm supposed to protect you. That's my job." He wanted to tell her he'd killed men for less, but even though he was dissatisfied with his chapter, he refused to spill details of club business.

Instead, he decided to change the subject. "You know that trip to Fayetteville I told you about?"

"Yes."

"I want us to make the trip permanent. I've asked to transfer chapters." He knew it was the best thing for both of them. However, he would also need to reach out to one of his friends in the Fayetteville chapter of the Kings to help pave the way because, unfortunately, getting Cecil's permission was only the first hurdle. The Fayetteville chapter would have to accept him into their club. "I've already got a good friend there. His name's Gypsy. You'll like him."

"You want me to move there with you?" she seemed shocked by the idea. "What if I get there and you change your mind about me?"

He cupped her face in his hands. "Not gonna happen. How many times do I have to tell you, you're it for me?" Hell, he'd tell her every day if he needed to.

"Take me to bed," she said, pulling her T-shirt off over her head.

Stake stood with Santana still wrapped around him. He'd spend every hour making love to her until he had to make the trip to San Antonio.

* * * *

Tiny cut the Harley's engine, and Santana climbed off. She couldn't believe she'd agreed to go swimming with him. The small lake on his grandfather's land had been one of their favorite places to go when they were growing up, but it had been a long time since she'd gone swimming. "It looks smaller," she noted, setting her helmet on the bike seat.

He snorted. "It's the same size, we're just bigger."

She stared up at the six-foot-seven-inch man and laughed. "Some of us bigger than others."

Tiny picked her up and tossed her over his shoulder. "You'll pay for that."

She laughed and beat her hands against his heavily muscled back. "Let me down!"

"Not gonna happen, squirt. I've waited years to toss you into this lake." He reached the water's edge and lifted her off his shoulder. As if she weighed nothing, he began to swing her back and forth over the water.

"Please, Tiny?" she begged. "I don't want to get my clothes wet."

"Nope." He released her and she flew through the air, her arms and legs waving wildly until she hit the surface. She sank under the water before coming up sputtering.

"I can't believe you just did that." She laughed again, splashing him as she waded back to the shore. It felt good to have her friend back. "You're an ass."

He kicked off his boots before pulling his shirt over his head.

"Jeez, Tiny." She couldn't believe the man in front of her was the same dork she'd been friends with for so many years. Not only was every inch of his torso and arms covered in black tats, but it appeared as though the man lived in a gym.

He flexed his muscles. "How do you think I get so much pussy? Sure as hell isn't my face."

"I've always liked your face. Well, at least until you started growing that beard. Seriously, you need to rethink that. You can't even see your dimples with all that pubic hair hiding how handsome you are." She decided to leave her shorts on over her swimsuit, but took her T-shirt off before laying it over a rock to dry.

"I like the beard," he grumbled before executing a shallow dive into the lake.

She dug a ponytail holder out of her pocket and took a few minutes to pile her hair on top of her head. When she was finished, she noticed him staring at her with his teeth clenched. The swimsuit she wore was old, but it wasn't any more revealing than a bra. Uncomfortable, she started to reach for her shirt.

"Don't," Tiny said. He pointed to her torso. "Gordon did that?"

She glanced down at the shallow cuts that had healed but were still pink. The bruises had turned to that sickly green color that she'd hoped to cover with a tan. "Yeah," she said, turning her back. She grabbed the shirt and pulled it on.

"Cannonball!" she yelled, racing toward the water. Her splash was lame, but she didn't know what else to do. She came up with a fake smile on her face, hoping to see a similar reaction from Tiny.

Unfortunately, he wasn't amused by her cannonball attempt. "Come on, it was a joke."

He reached out and yanked her into his massive arms, crushing her before she had a chance to fight him off. "I'm sorry."

Santana pushed against his shoulders, trying to break free. "You're squeezing me!"

He loosened his hold but didn't release her. "I'll make this up to you. I'll make everything up to you."

She started to make another joke about him trying to move in on Stake's territory, but all the pain Tiny had caused when he'd turned his back came pouring out of her. She began to hit her fists against his shoulders and head and he took it. "Damn you!"

Her breath caught at the expression of deep and profound sorrow on his ruggedly handsome face. She wrapped her arms around his neck when she realized the forced separation between them had been equally hard on him. She buried her face against his neck and started to cry. Within seconds, her tears turned to sobs, wracking full-bodied sobs that she'd never allowed herself to give into.

Tiny carried her out of the water and sat on the bank with Santana cradled in his arms. "I should've protected you, but I never have."

"You beat up Robby," she hiccupped as she reminded him.

"Afterward," he mumbled. "But I should've done something about your dad. I saw him hit you more than once, and all I did was stand there."

"You were a boy." She'd never blamed Tiny for not stepping in, only for walking away. Telling him what she'd figured out about her father wouldn't do either of them any good, so she kept her mouth shut as she dried her tears.

He cleared his throat. "The beard makes me look meaner than I really am," he confessed. "When we were younger, I couldn't wait for the day I could take Smash on."

She tugged on his beard. He was right. The combination of facial hair and tattoos made him look like one badass motherfucker. She knew he was no angel though. He liked to fight and had been kicked out of school more than once for brawling. "Do you still pick fights?" she asked, hoping to lighten his expression.

"Only when I know I can win." The corner of his mouth tipped up in a wicked grin.

Santana climbed off his lap and stretched out beside him. The sun felt good, and she still wanted to work on her tan. Plus, she doubted Stake would appreciate her sitting in another man's lap. She closed her eyes and let the warmth of the day envelope her. "I need to tell you a secret, but you can't tell anyone else." She didn't know if Stake's plans were a secret, but now that she'd reconnected with Tiny, she didn't want to leave without telling him.

He laid down next to her. "Okay."

"Stake asked Cecil if he could transfer to the Fayetteville chapter. He wants to take me as far away from Broken Ridge as we can get." She took a deep breath. "He said he's going to kill Gordon, but I can't let him do that because the police will know he's responsible. So, I'm going to do it," she confessed. "I need you to teach me how to shoot."

"No."

She opened her eyes and looked at Tiny when he said nothing more. "Please? If something happens to Stake because of me..." She let her words trail off as she shook her head. "I won't let that happen."

He rubbed his hands over his face. "I would do anything for you, but I can't teach you how to become someone like me and Stake. I won't."

The statement drove home what she'd often suspected but had never asked. Growing up in the club, she learned as a child not to ask questions, but she needed to know. "Have you and Stake killed people?"

"Don't ask me that," he replied.

Closing her eyes again, she thought back to the day the cops had come to their home and arrested her dad. At the time, she hadn't been upset or surprised that Smash had killed someone, only that he'd been caught, so it would make sense that Stake and even Tiny had, as well.

She decided to drop the conversation about Gordon. Although she hadn't given up on her plan to kill the bastard before Stake did, she wouldn't involve Tiny more than she already had. "Do you have a girlfriend?"

He let out a loud grunt. "A different one almost every night," he said, a chuckle in his voice. "The ladies love my cock."

Santana reached over and slapped him hard on the chest. Despite Tiny trying to get into her pants as a young teenager, she'd always thought of him more like a brother. "Gross. I don't need to hear that."

"It's true," he said unapologetically. "They also like to ride my face." He held up his hands in a defensive position as soon as he said it, knowing she'd try to whack him again.

"Nasty! You're a pig like the rest of them." She squeezed her legs together, remembering the first time Stake had eaten her pussy. *Fuck.* "Did Stake say what time he'd be home?"

Laughing, Tiny rose to his feet and headed for the water. "You'd better cool that hot little body down 'cuz he won't be back 'til late."

Dammit, had she been so obvious? With a sigh of resignation, she followed Tiny back into the lake.

Chapter Seven

The minute Tiny pulled up to Stake's house, he turned off his bike and reached in his pocket. "My goddamn cell's been vibrating since we left the lake," he said. He stared at the display, and his dark blond eyebrows drew together. "It's Prez." He glanced back at Santana. "Sorry, sweetheart, but I need to take this."

"No problem." She climbed off the bike before setting the helmet on the seat. "I'll be inside."

She hoisted herself onto the back porch, wondering why Stake had never bothered to build stairs. The porch wasn't high off the ground, probably only two feet or so, but while it was an easy step up for Stake, she was only five-foot-five.

She used her key to enter the house before retrieving a bottle of water from the refrigerator. Swimming had been fun after she'd recovered from her meltdown, and she'd managed to get some nice color.

Tiny knocked before entering. "I've gotta go out for a while."

"Problem?" She asked, opening the fridge to hand him a bottle of water.

"Business, but I should only be gone a few hours."

She sighed. Stake had left money for grocery shopping, but Tiny was supposed to go with her. She eyed the envelope of cash on the table. It was stupid, but she'd really looked forward to shopping without worrying about the total. Stake had been very clear that she was to load up on junk food because he enjoyed eating shit while he watched baseball on TV. "Will you be back in time for dinner? I thought I'd make meatloaf."

He groaned and rubbed his flat stomach. "Hell yeah, I'll be back. I fuckin' love meatloaf."

"Good." She finished her water and tossed the empty bottle into the recycle bin she'd created out of an old cardboard box lined with a trash bag.

"You have your phone?" he asked.

"Yep." Stake had insisted on buying her a new phone. She unplugged it from the charger on the counter.

Tiny walked over and gave her a peck on the forehead. "Sorry about this. Stake'll probably kill me for leaving you alone, but at this point, I'm more afraid of Cecil."

She waved off his concerns. "I'll be fine. I've spent most of my life taking care of myself. I'm sure I can handle it for a few hours."

His expression darkened. He shook his head before giving her another friendly kiss. "I like brown gravy with my meatloaf. You do it that way?"

"I can." She didn't tell him it had been years since she'd had enough money to buy the hamburger required for meatloaf, let alone splurge on gravy.

"Stay safe," he called as he walked out of the door.

She waited until she could no longer hear the sound of his Harley before running to the bedroom to change into dry clothes and brush out her hair. She grabbed the extra set of keys and the envelope before heading out of the house.

Behind the wheel of Stake's truck, she took several deep breaths. It had been close to three years since their old piece of shit car had finally given up the fight, but she assumed driving was something you never really forgot how to do. "You've got this," she repeated over and over as she started the pickup and pulled out onto the road.

The drive went so well that she turned on the radio on the outskirts of town. She was almost to downtown when flashing lights in her rearview mirror caught her attention. Her immediate reaction was to stiffen and glance down at her speedometer. She wasn't speeding, so what the fuck? Pulling to the side of the road, she turned off the engine and started searching her purse for her driver's license.

"Fuck me," she groaned when she spotted Robby Langers walking toward the truck in the driver's side mirror. She hadn't spoken to Robby since the day she'd heard his douchebag jock friends talking smack about her. She held out her license and the registration she'd retrieved from the glove box. "I wasn't speeding," she said before he could speak.

Robby leaned his forearm against the door and stared straight at her tits. "Looking good." When Santana flinched, he held up his hands and took a step back. "It was just a compliment. Don't stab me." He started to laugh like he'd told the funniest joke ever.

A 'fuck you' was on the tip of her tongue, but she held it back. Robby was the kind of dick who would arrest her at the slightest provocation. "Why'd you stop me?"

Sobering, he glanced down at her license. "I haven't seen you drive for a while. Thought it best to make sure you were still legal." He handed her license and registration back. "And to give you a warning. Folks in town aren't happy that you tried to file a false police report on Sheriff Gordon. You might watch your back while you're in town."

She rolled her eyes and bit her bottom lip. "Can I leave?"

He eyed her for several moments before slapping his palm against the side of the truck. "I wasn't kidding when I said you looked good. I'd ask you out, but I heard you've shacked up with that piece of shit biker."

Finished with the conversation, she started the truck and pulled back onto the road without a reply. She couldn't believe that slime had the nerve to think she would ever go out with him again.

By the time she parked in front of the grocery store, most of her enthusiasm had waned. She tossed the keys into her purse and confirmed she'd grabbed the envelope of cash before going inside.

Barb, the not so friendly cashier, stopped chatting with a customer to stare at her as Santana fought to untangle a cart. She did her best to ignore the whispered gossip that floated around her as she made her way through the aisles. With absolutely no appetite, she found it difficult to shop, but she loaded the cart with two boxes of cereal, chips, Coke and Grape Crush before heading to the meat department. One thing Stake had made clear since she'd begun to cook was that he required meat, and lots of it, at every meal. She thoughtfully picked up enough hamburger, steaks and pork chops and chicken to last the two weeks they'd still be in Broken Ridge.

By the time she finished, she could barely maneuver the cart to the check-out lane. As she started to unload her groceries, she caught Barb staring at her. "Is there a problem?"

Barb gestured to the food piled on the conveyor belt. "You have enough money to pay for all this?" She clucked her tongue. "Looks like you came out ahead after stabbing Pete."

Tired of the bullshit, Santana dropped a twelve pack of Coke back into the cart. "You know what? Fuck this. If you don't want to sell me groceries, just say so, otherwise, shut your goddamn mouth, and do your job."

Barb gasped and crossed her arms over her saggy tits. "How dare you speak to me that way, you piece of trash."

Santana was trying to calculate how long it would take for her to drive to the next town with a grocery store when a middle-aged man she'd never seen moved to stand next to Barb.

"Is there a problem?" he asked the cashier.

Before Barb could open her big mouth, Santana answered the question. "Yes, there is. I've been shopping at this store my entire life, and this woman has treated me like I didn't exist for most of those years." She gestured to the mounds of food waiting to be scanned. "Now, I'm trying to buy all this, and your employee feels the need to call me trash and spout her fucking mouth about something she knows nothing about."

The man looked at Barb. "Is that the truth?"

"She's the one who stabbed Sheriff Gordon," Barb replied. "We don't need her kind in here."

The handsome man scratched his jaw. "Well, since you don't own the store, I can't see where that's your place to determine." His hands moved to his hips. "I think it's best you take the rest of the day off while I try and figure out if you still have a job come morning."

"You can't talk to me like that. I've been here for over thirty years. Bob won't let you just come in here and fire me."

The man shrugged. "Maybe not, but he hired me to manage the place, and that's what I'm doing." He didn't try to hide his animosity toward Barb, and Santana could barely keep the smile of satisfaction off her face.

With a final harrumph, Barb squeezed past the man, waving her finger in the air. "This isn't over. I'm calling Bob," she said as she walked toward the back of the store.

"Sorry about that." The man rolled up his shirtsleeves and began scanning.

"Thank you," Santana said as she finished unloading the cart.

The man smiled at her and held out his hand. "I'm Keith, the new manager Bob hired when he decided to retire to Iowa to be closer to his grandchildren."

"Santana," she said, shaking his hand. She was genuinely amazed that Keith was being so kind. "You must be new in town."

He grinned. "Yeah, but it's not my first small town. Ensuring a store stays in the black is nothing compared to navigating the local gossips."

She liked Keith so much she was tempted to tell him she wasn't the woman Barb made her out to be, but she got the feeling he already suspected that. By the time her groceries were sacked and paid for, her mood had lifted considerably. "Thanks again," she said with a smile.

"You come back, and if you ever have another problem with any of our employees, ask for me."

"I will." Santana pushed the cart toward the automatic doors. The moment they opened, she froze.

Her breath left her body in a whoosh as she stared into Pete Gordon's eyes. He was sitting behind the wheel of his Sheriff's car staring straight at her.

With a hand to her chest, she stumbled backward, heedless of the display of greeting cards she'd knocked over. "No. No," she gasped as she felt herself falling.

* * * *

Stake handed Charity the bi-monthly pregnancy test all the girls were required to take. "Make sure you keep this up once I'm gone," he told her. The tests were his requirement, not the club's, and he paid for them out of his own pocket. He seriously doubted whoever took over for him would care enough about the girls' health to do the same.

"I can't believe you're leaving us," Charity whined as she opened the bathroom door.

Charity was one of the few whores who remained clean despite the Kings' new incentive program. She was a good kid. Knowing the Kings in Fayetteville also ran a small prostitution business, he scribbled his phone number on piece of paper and handed it to her. "If you decide to get the fuck out of San Antonio, give me a call, and I'll get you a job in Fayetteville."

"Arkansas?" she laughed.

"Hey, don't knock it. The scenery is gorgeous, green as the eye can see." He looked forward to cutting the grass, something he'd never had to do before. His phone rang, pulling his attention away from Charity. One look at the display and he grinned. "Hey, bug."

"This is Keith Oberman, manager of the Pick and Save. I'm sorry, but your number was the only one programmed into Santana's phone."

Stake's heart stopped beating at the mention of Santana's name. "What's happened?"

"Well, she's had a bit of a spell, and she's currently sitting in my office because I don't think she's coherent enough to drive herself home. I was wondering if you'd be able to come and get her?"

"Hang on a second." Stake knocked on the bathroom door. "Gotta go," he told Charity as he left the studio apartment. "What do you mean a spell?" he asked Keith.

Keith cleared his throat. "The sheriff was parked outside the store when she started to leave. She…umm, well, she didn't handle it well. Unfortunately, he's still here, which is why I brought her back to my office."

"I'm an hour out." *Fuck. Where the hell was Tiny?* "Was she alone?"

"Yeah. I'd drive her, but I sent Barb home earlier, and no one else is on shift who can run the register."

Stake climbed on his bike. "I'll be there as soon as I can. Whatever you do, don't let her leave, even if Gordon isn't parked out front."

"Okay," Keith agreed. "She has a bunch of groceries, but I'll put the refrigerated items in the cooler until you get here."

"Thanks." Stake hung up and roared away from the curb. Tiny was going to fucking die when he got hold of him.

Fifty minutes later, he parked his bike next to the pickup. There was no sign of Gordon, which probably saved the bastard from a trip to the morgue. The motherfucker deserved to die, and Stake's patience with his Prez was running out.

As soon as he entered the store, a man behind the checkout counter, stopped what he was doing and walked toward Stake. "Stake?" he asked, holding out his hand.

"Yeah. Where is she?" He appreciated the man's kindness, but he needed to see his woman.

"Straight back, first door on the right. I'll have one of the stockers help you with the groceries."

Stake wanted to tell him he didn't give a fuck about the groceries, but simply nodded before taking off. He jogged down the aisle and pushed through the swinging door. He turned right and entered the office.

He found Santana sitting in a comfortable-looking desk chair with her hands fisted in her lap. Instead of looking distressed, she appeared to be pissed.

Santana jumped to her feet. "Get me out of here," she demanded.

Before she could blow by him, Stake hooked an arm around her waist and pulled her into a tight embrace. "I'm so sorry," he whispered against her ear as he tried to wrap his body around her.

"Not your fault," she said without emotion. "I just want to go home. I'm fine to drive, and I tried to tell Keith that, but he took my keys and said I couldn't have them back until you got here."

Stake cradled her face in his hands. "Where's Tiny? He should've been here for you."

She shrugged. "Cecil called, and Tiny had to leave." She shook her head. "I didn't tell him I was going to shop, anyway." Tears formed in her gorgeous hazel eyes and began to trickle down her cheeks. "I was so excited about shopping." She closed her eyes. "I was stupid."

He dried her tears and crushed her against his chest once more. "You weren't stupid, just reckless."

"I hate this town."

"So do I, bug." Fuck the two weeks he still had left on his deal with Cecil. He needed to get her away from Broken Ridge as soon as possible.

* * * *

Santana woke to two deep voices arguing on the back porch. She sat up and rubbed her eyes. By the time they'd arrived back at the house, she hadn't put up a fight when Stake had suggested she lay down.

She swung her legs over the side of the mattress and looked at the clock. It was nearly eight, no wonder her stomach was growling. She pulled on her shorts and shuffled toward the commotion on the porch. From the sound of it, Tiny and Stake were really going at it—something she knew was her fault.

"I thought I could trust you!" Stake bellowed.

"You can. I'd give my life for that woman," Tiny argued.

She opened the door. "Stop!" she screamed. "It's not Tiny's fault. It's mine. I told you that."

Stake's mouth snapped shut as he turned to stare at her. His hair was sticking out as if he'd dragged his fingers through it a thousand times since she'd laid down. "How're you feeling?"

"I was fine, but now I'm getting a headache from all the yelling." She glanced from Tiny to Stake. "You're the only two people in the world I care about. Please don't do this."

"I'm sorry," Tiny mumbled, appearing genuinely upset by the whole situation. "No matter how hard I try, I keep fucking things up."

Santana moved to wrap her arms around her friend. "I had one of the best mornings of my life today. You did that. You gave me that."

Tiny grinned down at her. "I think your man's getting a little jealous."

She looked over her shoulder at Stake. "Don't let him intimidate you. He knows I only have eyes for him."

"That doesn't mean I enjoy watching you touch another man," Stake countered.

She took a step back and was immediately pulled into Stake's arms. "Are you hungry? I can put a couple of steaks on the grill," he asked.

She nodded. "I'm starving."

"I'm gonna get out of here. Are you still coming to the wedding tomorrow night?" Tiny asked.

"I don't know if that's a good idea," Stake began.

"We'll be there." Although she didn't want to attend the celebration, she knew Stake would hate himself if he missed out on a brother's big day.

Stake gave her a squeeze. "Maybe," he told Tiny.

"You know Mad Dog thinks you're the shit. He'll be pissed if you don't come." Tiny kissed Santana's cheek, despite the growl from Stake. "That's the last time I let you down. I promise."

"You didn't let me down, so I wish you'd stop saying stuff like that." Seeing Gordon had knocked her on her ass, literally, but she refused to blame Tiny for it. She hadn't mentioned to Stake that she'd been pulled over by Robby, and didn't intend to. Honestly, she didn't care to step foot in the town of Broken Ridge ever again, and if they were truly leaving in a few weeks, she saw no reason she'd have to.

Chapter Eight

Stake was loading beer into the cooler when Santana walked into the kitchen. "Leave room for the apple salad," she reminded him.

He glanced over his shoulder and narrowed his gaze at the faded dress that hung off her shoulders like a sack. *Shit.* He never thought he'd be the kind of man to criticize a woman's dress, but, hell, the damn thing made her look thirty pounds heavier.

"What?" she asked, peering down at herself.

He stood up and kicked the lid of the cooler shut. "Where'd you get that dress?" Christ, how did you tell a woman she didn't look good and still ensure her pussy was available afterward?

"I've had it for a long time." She bit her bottom lip. "You don't like it?"

He shrugged. "I was hoping for something a little sexier." He walked over and set his hands on her hips. "I want every man at the reception to want to be me." He gave her a soft kiss. "Does that make me a dog?"

"Yes." She grinned. "The only dresses I have that are sexy belonged to my mom, and I don't want everyone to know I took her clothes."

Despite being roughly the same size, Santana was a hell of a lot more shapely than Ellie. "It's been years. I don't think anyone will even notice you're wearing something of Ellie's." He took her hand and led her into the bedroom. "May I?" he asked, gesturing to the closet.

With a sigh, Santana pulled away and sat on the edge of the bed. "I don't think you'll find anything that'll fit. My boobs and ass are bigger than mom's."

He realized she saw her curves as a negative. Is that why she'd dressed in the sack? "Ellie's body didn't hold a candle to yours, bug." He started through the clothes, searching for something stretchy. Making Santana try on something that didn't fit would blow up in his face. He came to a mint green dress that seemed to have some give. Better yet, it was short and he could imagine the view of her tits through the keyhole neckline. He pulled it out and held it up. "I'd fuckin' die to see you in this one."

She shook her head. "That's not going to fit me."

He carried the dress over and knelt in front of Santana. "I promise it will." He laid it beside her. "Just think how easy it'll be for me to finger your pussy in this one." He reached down and began to gather the long material of the dress she wore, rolling it up until he had a view of her underwear. He leaned in and scraped his teeth over the nylon that covered her pussy. "And eat your pussy."

She gasped when he pulled her underwear to the side and slid his tongue between the lips of her pussy. "Please try the green one?" he asked before sucking on her clit.

Moaning, she buried her fingers in his hair as he continued to taste her. "Yes."

He wasn't sure what she was saying yes to, the dress or the attention to her pussy, but he felt satisfied she'd do as asked. Inserting two fingers to pump in and out of her core, he continued to suck her clit until her body began to buck against his mouth.

"Oh God!" she cried as she climaxed.

He removed his fingers and gathered her juices on his tongue as she rode out her orgasm.

Falling back onto the bed, she started to laugh. "That's one way to change my mind."

* * * *

Santana scowled at Stake as she did her best to climb out of the truck without flashing her pussy to everyone gathered in front of the small country church. "I'm going to kill you for this."

Laughing, Stake walked over and lifted her off the seat before lowering her to the graveled parking lot. "I'll carry you anywhere you need to go if you'll admit you feel damn sexy in that dress."

Despite the short length of the dress, the fact that half her tits were on display and the four-inch heels, it was the expression on Stake's face that made her feel sexy, but he didn't need to know that. "I'm going to fall in these shoes and make a fool of myself," she grumbled as he led her across the parking lot.

"I've got ya, bug." He tightened his hold on her waist as they joined the mingling crowd of people.

The small church didn't have air conditioning, so most people had decided to wait until the wedding was due to start to go inside. She glanced up at Stake, feeling proud to be his date for the evening. Although he still wore his black leather cut, he'd dressed in a crisp white dress shirt and a pair of black jeans with his hair tied back in a short ponytail at the nape of his neck. He made her swoon each time she caught a glimpse of him. She remembered how much she'd longed to be the woman on his arm while growing up, and through a twist of fate, there she was, standing next to him as his hand rested on her ass.

When people began to file into the church, Stake broke away from the conversation to smile down at her. "Ready?"

She returned his smile and nodded. Before she could take a step, someone behind her lifted her off the ground. Her gaze immediately went to Stake, but he simply scowled. "Put my woman down, Tiny."

Tiny did as he was told. "You look beautiful," he told her.

She wanted to tell her friend that she felt a bit like the tramp she'd always considered her mother to be, but she held her tongue. "Thanks."

Once again, Stake settled a proprietary hand on her ass and urged her forward. She knew Stake wasn't really jealous of Tiny, but the two seemed to enjoy picking at each other.

They were ushered to the groom's side of the church about halfway down, and she sighed in relief when she realized she'd be seated between Tiny and Stake. With tall men on both sides and another giant of a biker in front of her, she doubted she'd see much of the ceremony. "I feel like I need a stack of phone books to sit on," she said, crossing her arms.

Stake looked down and grinned before reaching out and running a finger over her exposed breasts. "You can always sit on my lap."

She licked her lips in an attempt to tease him as much as he was teasing her. "Think you could handle my ass in your lap for the entire ceremony?"

"Shit." He removed his hand and covered his erection with his program seconds before an elderly woman sat beside him.

Santana recognized the woman as one of the club member's old lady but couldn't remember her name. Didn't matter. Even though she now understood why the club families had turned their back, she still didn't understand why they had all turned a blind eye to the way her parents had treated her.

Stake leaned forward and said something to the brother on the other side of the woman.

"Don't look now, but someone's staring daggers," Tiny said in her ear.

Stake had already informed her that Rachel would most likely attend the celebration, so she'd prepared herself in advance. "Rachel?"

"How'd you guess?" Tiny chuckled. "She's a piece of work. Thinks she's better than everyone, but she spreads her legs like a fucking whore when she drinks."

Santana slapped Tiny's arm. Although she loved to hear it from someone other than Stake, she doubted a church was the proper place for such a conversation. "Later," she whispered.

Remembering what Stake had told her about standing up for herself with the other women of the club, Santana turned until she made eye contact with Rachel. She didn't drop her gaze until Rachel looked away. *Bitch.*

Although he was still talking to the club member, Stake reached out and rested his palm on Santana's upper thigh. Had he known Rachel was staring?

Tiny chuckled, obviously reading Santana's mind. "That's for my benefit," he told her.

She rolled her eyes. "You two are getting out of hand."

"Naw," Tiny said. "Stake's been top stud for too long, it's time he stepped down and let a real man take the lead."

Stake broke away from his conversation to stare at Tiny. "Why're you pushin' my buttons? You have a death wish?"

"No, but you have Santana, and I've already told you that if you cheat on her, I'll kill ya, so with you off the market, I'm all set to swoop in and take your place."

"Yeah, like you need more pussy," Stake scoffed.

A throat cleared directly behind them, and Stake glanced over his shoulder before moving his hand higher on Santana's thigh. "Mrs. Johnson," he acknowledged with a dip of his chin.

Tiny nudged Santana in the ribs with his elbow as his eyes rounded. Santana grinned but didn't turn around to confirm Mrs. Johnson's presence. Alice Johnson had been an old woman when Santana had been a child, so she couldn't imagine how she was still alive.

The music started, and they watched as three bridesmaids walked down the aisle on the arm of groomsmen. Like Stake, every man in the bridal party, except the best man, was dressed in white shirts, black jeans and their cuts. She assumed the best man must be Mad Dog's brother.

When the wedding march began, everyone got to their feet. Santana couldn't see a damn thing, but she supposed it didn't matter since she'd never met the bride anyway. However, she did have an incredible view of Stake's ass, which more than made up for it.

* * * *

Stake parked in the lot in front of the clubhouse. "Don't flirt with Tiny in front of other people."

Santana rolled her eyes. "It's not me, it's him. I think he's just trying to piss you off."

"I know he's full of shit, but everyone else doesn't." He got out of the truck and walked around to the passenger door. He didn't give a fuck what people thought of him, but Santana had already had a rough go of it, and the last thing she needed was to overhear the typical bullshit gossip. He opened Santana's door. "And, don't put up with any of Rachel's shit tonight, especially because I'm sure she'll be drinking."

"I know, I already had to stare her down in church." She cracked her knuckles before pounding one fist against the palm of her other hand. "I'm ready, coach."

He couldn't help but smile. Goddamn, she made him smile more than anyone ever had. He pulled her into his arms and kissed her deeply as he lifted her from the pickup. Before releasing her, he ground his cock against her. "I haven't seen you drunk before. You get horny?"

She shrugged. "I've never been drunk before, so I have no idea. I've always been afraid to lose control because I never wanted to be like mamma." She tapped her finger against her chin.

"It might be good for you to lose control for a change. You know I'll protect you," Stake said.

"Yeah." She seemed to consider it a moment longer before nodding. "Okay, I'm going to let loose, get drunk and see where the night takes me as long as you promise you won't abandon me."

Fucking at any time was great, but there was something about a hard, drunk fuck that couldn't be beat in his opinion. It was a good thing he'd made her leave the underwear at home. *Shit.* Just the thought of fucking her hard had all his blood flowing from his brain to his dick. "You know I'd never leave you. So, drink all you want, but not too much that you can't wrap your legs around me later."

A car pulled up beside them, prompting him to release her. He opened the tailgate and lifted the cooler. "Can you make it without holding on to me?"

"I'll try." She started across the parking lot with Stake close behind her.

"Damn, your ass looks good in that dress," he noted.

She grinned over her shoulder and attempted to give her sweet ass an exaggerated wiggle, but the movement caused her to lose her footing on the gravel. Stake dropped the cooler and caught her before she tumbled to the ground.

Laughing, he left the cooler where it was and carried her the rest of the way across the parking lot. "Will you be safe here until I get back?"

Her cheeks flushed, she nodded without looking at him.

"Hey." He tilted her chin up. "You're fine. I like it when you let loose with me."

"I almost made a fool of myself in front of everyone," she mumbled.

"So? Other than me and Tiny, who the fuck here do you give a shit about?" He'd never understand why women were always so concerned about what other people thought.

Sadness filled her beautiful eyes.

Fuck. He hadn't meant to sound so pissed off. It was a flaw he had to really work on with her, not because she'd asked him to, but because she'd had enough verbal abuse in her life without him adding to it.

"It's not that I care about anyone else specifically, but I've had a lifetime of being humiliated around these people. I guess I want to show them I'm different now," she explained.

Tiny passed by with Stake's wayward cooler in his hands. "You dropped this."

"Thanks. Take it over with the others, would you?" Stake asked.

Tiny looked between Santana and Stake before nodding. "Sure."

Stake led Santana over to stand in a shaded spot on the side of the building. He put his back to the clubhouse and pulled her against his chest, facing outward. "See that blonde over there talking to Cecil?"

"Yes."

"He's fucking her, and she's young enough to be his granddaughter. My aunt doesn't know, but everyone else here does, including her best friend." He scanned the crowd again. "Do you know Iggy?"

"Kind of."

"Well, Iggy's some kind of sick sex freak who is hard all the time but refuses to fuck because he thinks it's gross. Instead, he likes to get head while sitting in the clubhouse for anyone to see."

"That is gross. Why're you telling me this?" she asked.

"Because I'm trying to make you understand that everyone here has problems that they would probably consider humiliating if they knew everyone else knew. The fact that Ellie was a drunk and Smash raised his hand to you more than he ever should have, isn't something for you to worry about. First of all, that's Smash and Ellie's shame, not yours, and secondly, it was a long time ago. Even if it wasn't, these people aren't worth worrying about. We'll be gone in another two weeks, and with luck, you'll never see most of them again." He spotted his mom walking across the lawn toward them. "Christ. Here comes my mom. Don't pay attention to anything she has to say."

"I wondered where the two of you were." Stake's mom stopped in front of them and eyed Santana warily. "It's nice to see you again," she told Santana.

"You remember my mom, Peggy, don't you?" Stake asked, his lips brushing Santana's ear.

"Yes. How've you been?" Santana asked.

"Well, I'd be better if I could get my son to come by and change my oil like I've asked him to do for the last month." She propped her hands on her hips and stared daggers at Stake.

"I told you when you asked that you needed to take it into town and have it done, or have that worthless piece of shit living with you do it," Stake argued. He'd spent more than half of his life trying to please his mom, but by the time he'd reached his twenties, he'd come to the conclusion that nothing would be enough for her. Other than a few times a year, he didn't even bother going by the house he'd grown up in because he never knew who he was going to find shacked up with his mom.

"Jerry has a bad back," she argued right back. "I told you that."

"I don't give a fuck. I'm not changing your damn oil, so stop asking, and take care of it yourself."

Peggy turned her attention to Santana. "Do you see how poorly my worthless son treats me?"

Santana straightened and squared her shoulders. "From what I understand, you deserve it," she shot back.

Pride and something else, he couldn't put a finger on, filled him. Had Santana just stuck up for him against his mom? Everyone in the club knew Peggy Wills as Queen Bitch. Because of her close relationship to Cecil, his mom had always felt she could do or say anything she wanted without reproach, and she'd gotten away with it for the most part, until two seconds earlier.

"Watch yourself, sweetheart," Peggy sneered.

Santana stepped out of Stake's embrace, putting herself nose to nose with Peggy. "I could say the same to you. I haven't forgotten the way you laughed when you saw Smash take a willow branch to me at the Easter picnic."

"You were a brat," Peggy said in an attempt to excuse her actions.

"He beat me until I was fucking bloody!" Santana screamed, drawing attention.

As much as he wanted Santana to get her anger out, he stepped between the two women, knowing she'd only feel worse if she realized others were listening. "That's enough," he told his mom. "Go on back to your beer and Jerry, and leave us the fuck alone."

Peggy shook her head. "Trash. Just like her parents."

Stake wrapped his hand around his mother's throat. "Give me a fucking reason to snap your neck," he warned.

Eye wide with shock, his mom sputtered, "Stake? What has she done to you?"

Stake squeezed, making his hold increasingly uncomfortable but not tight enough to really hurt her. "She's taught me how it feels to be loved," he ground out. "And I will kill you if you so much as look in her direction. You got me, bitch?"

"What the hell's going on over here?" Cecil demanded.

Stake released his grip on his mom's throat, but didn't back away. "Stay out of it, Prez. This is between me and Mom."

"What the fuck's wrong with you, boy?" Cecil growled. "That's your mother."

"We both know she's never been a mother to me, so there's no way in hell I'm gonna stand by and let her hurl insults at Santana." He stared at Cecil, ready to take the old man on if he needed. "Take your sister, and tell her to either get the hell out of here or stay away from me and Santana until we can move the fuck out of this town."

"Stake," Santana said, putting her hand on his arm. "Let's just go."

He reached back and hooked his arm around her waist, pulling her against his side. "No. Last I checked, I'm the one with the cut, not my mother." He stared at his mom again, willing her to walk the fuck away because he had an entire arsenal of shit he'd held inside for too long, and it was begging to get out.

"We need to talk," Cecil said.

"Yeah, we do," Stake agreed. He needed to call Gypsy and find out how things were progressing on his end. Transfers didn't happen automatically, and he prayed the Fayetteville brothers liked him enough to accept him as one of their own. "Find me in a few hours," he told Cecil. "In the meantime, get her out of here."

"Are you going to let him talk to me like that?" Peggy asked, still rubbing her throat.

"Enough," Cecil said, steering his sister away from Stake and Santana.

"Shit." Santana hugged him. "That was bad."

He shrugged. "That was a long time coming."

"Yeah," she agreed.

After turning to pull her against his chest, he leaned down and kissed her. "No one's ever stood up for me like that." God, he'd already believed he'd fallen in love with her, but that one action had sealed his fate. "I love you," he admitted for the first time.

Tears filled Santana's gorgeous eyes as she smiled up at him. "Yeah?"

"Yeah," he confirmed.

"I love you, too."

His heart swelled at the proclamation. He'd known she'd first fallen in love with the idea of him, but after she'd not only witnessed his exchange with his mom, but she'd supported him, he knew she loved the real him. "I'm not the kind of man most women want to make a life with. I live hard, and I do things that aren't always within the law, but I will cherish you until the day I die."

"I'm good with that," she said, drying her tears.

* * * *

Santana covered her ears as Stake aimed his gun at the target and fired. "Yes!" she pumped her fists into the air when the bullet pierced the center of the red bull's-eye. For as long as she could remember, the club had held shooting competitions whenever they got together, and she'd always loved to watch Stake shoot. Not only was he the best, but there had always been something so sexy about watching his muscles as he took aim and fired.

Stake gave his brothers a wicked grin before walking back to her.

She threw her arms around his neck and pulled his head down for a deep kiss. "You're still the best," she whispered against his lips.

"Yeah, well, it doesn't hurt to remind the young'uns about that on occasion." He flattened his palms against her ears as Iggy stepped up to the line to shoot.

She wasn't surprised when Iggy's shot barely hit the target. The man was so drunk he could barely stand. "Why do you guys let Iggy shoot in that condition?"

"Because he's always in that condition," Stake replied. "If we don't let him compete, he shoots shit up once he gets really sauced. Better to have him do it under a controlled environment."

"Last one," Cecil announced.

Tiny made a show of kissing his 9mm before taking aim.

"He's always been a showoff," Santana said.

"He's good," Stake said before covering her ears again.

Tiny's shot hit just below Stake's. "Damn good," Stake said with a shake of his head.

Santana spotted Rachel eyeing them and pressed her body against Stake's. "Kiss me."

With a wicked grin, he bent and covered her mouth with his. She opened for his thrusting tongue and delighted when she felt his hands grope her ass. *Take that, Rachel.*

* * * *

With Santana seated in his lap, Stake pulled out his phone. "I need to call Gypsy before my meeting with Cecil."

"You want me to get us another beer while you do that?" she asked.

"No. I want you right where you are." The last thing she needed was someone else confronting her, and Rachel had been circling like a vulture for the last twenty minutes. He rested his hand on her hip and made the call.

"Hey, ya bastard, how've you been?" Gypsy answered.

Stake grinned. Gypsy was one of the few people who could get away with calling him that particular name, but then Gypsy was a bastard as well. "Typical shit," he grumbled.

"Still have that lady you told me about?"

"Hell, yes, and I'm not about to let her get away, so you need to give me some good news." He moved his hand to cup her ass, reminding himself, once again, why he needed to get the fuck away from Broken Ridge.

"Fifty-fifty. Some of the brothers are worried you'll come in and try to take over," Gypsy explained.

"I don't wanna take over anything. I'm trying to get away from drama, not create it. All I need is my ride, my woman and a steady gig that'll help pay the bills."

Santana leaned in and gave him a kiss, slipping her tongue inside to tease him before pulling back. "I need another beer, and I think I'll look for Tiny while I'm at it," she told Stake.

He nodded and gave her ass a squeeze before releasing her. "Go ahead and grab me a fresh one, too, and if you don't see Tiny right away, come back."

"Will do," she said before walking off. She'd taken off her heels, and although her legs didn't look as sexy, she was much steadier on her feet.

"Sorry about that," he told Gypsy. "Now that I can speak freely, I need you to share with your club why I need to get Santana away from this fucked up town. I'd rather the brothers didn't tell their old ladies about the details for Santana's sake, but I think it's important they understand the situation."

"Thought you said you were gonna kill the fat fuck."

"I am, but Cecil hasn't given the green light yet, so I need to be smart about it. I don't mind defying my prez on this, but the cops are still patrolling the stretch of road in front of Gordon's place on a regular basis. I may want the fucker dead, but I won't risk leaving Santana alone if I get sloppy."

"Makes sense. You know, the offer's still open if you want me to come down and take care of that problem for you. I don't know him so I wouldn't even be on the cops' radar."

"I appreciate the offer, but if anyone's going to take the risk, it needs to be me." He still cursed himself that he hadn't arrived at Santana's house earlier on the night of the attack. Had he found Gordon, the fucker would already be dead and his body dumped in a pit somewhere.

"Well, let me know if you change your mind. Found a place you might want to look at when you get here. It's not fancy, but it has potential and you said privacy was more important than the house, and this one's as private as they come. Sits well off the road and is completely surrounded by trees. Hell, if you didn't know it was there, you'd probably never find it."

"Sounds perfect," Stake agreed. "How much land?"

"Only thirty-two acres, but the closest neighbors are damn near a mile down the road."

"Is the house livable?" He wouldn't put Santana back into a home like the one she'd grown up in.

"It's a big farmhouse, so I'm sure you'll need to do some updating, but the structure's solid and it's had a new roof within the last two years. I figured you could work on the rooms a little at a time until you're satisfied. You're basically paying for the land so any improvements will only make the property value go up."

Stake grinned. Gypsy sounded like a real estate agent, which made sense since he was the brother who'd negotiated the Fayetteville chapter's headquarters. It had once been a summer camp, but the Kings had purchased it and turned it into one hell of a compound. "Send me some pictures, and I'll wire you enough money to hold the place until we get there."

"Sounds like a plan, and I'll talk to the brothers again. It'll help once you get out here. Although the older members remember you, some of the new patches have never met you."

"I understand." He hung up the phone before shoving it back into his pocket. Getting to his feet, he decided to find Santana and make sure Tiny was with her before he left for his meeting with Cecil.

He found Santana standing near the coolers. "Hey, bug."

She smiled. "I didn't find Tiny, so I've been waiting to get to the beer."

He glanced at his brothers who were standing around the coolers bullshitting. "You should've asked them to move."

Biting her lower lip, she wrinkled her nose. "I didn't want to do that. I kept hoping they'd wander off."

Stake chuckled. "They'll never get far from the beer." He took her hand and led her to the gathering. "The lady needs another beer," he announced, nudging Grips out of the way.

The brother moved to the side, creating an opening for Santana. "Sorry," he mumbled.

She opened the cooler and removed three bottles. "Thank you," she said as she returned to Stake's side. She handed one of the beers to him. "I got two for me in case I need another while you're in the meeting."

"Good idea." He hooked his arm around her neck and rubbed the ice cold bottle against the keyhole opening in her dress. She shivered at the contact, but he was pleased to see her nipples harden against the thin material. Unable to resist, he transferred the bottle to his other hand and ran his fingers across the soft skin of her tits. "Shit. We'd better find Tiny before I say to hell with the meeting and fuck you against the pickup."

Tiny stepped out of the shadows and headed straight for them. "Looking for me?"

Stake was drunk enough that he didn't stop fondling Santana's breasts at the question. "Yeah. I need you to keep Santana company while I talk to Cecil."

"Would you stop trying to molest my best friend right in front of me!" Tiny winced. "Shit. I can't believe I said that." He looked at Santana. "I'm sorry."

Santana fisted her hand and punched Tiny in the arm. "You do not get to apologize for trying to defend my honor." She stood on her tiptoes and gave Stake a deep kiss. "Go have your meeting while I set my friend straight on a few things."

Stake grinned. "I was dreading this meeting, but now I think I'd rather be me than you," he told Tiny.

"Yeah, I think I might agree," Tiny replied.

* * * *

Settled in twin lawn chairs on the outskirts of the party, Santana took another drink of her beer. She was already tipsy, and Tiny's insistence that she share sips from his bottle of whiskey would no doubt have her drunk in no time. She eyed her friend warily. He'd been quiet since they'd found the spot to sit, and she could tell something was bothering him. "Okay, I've been patient long enough. What's wrong?"

Tiny upended his bottle and poured an ungodly amount of alcohol down his throat. "You're leaving."

"Yeah." She suddenly understood. "I'm sorry, but this town, the people, they'll never see me as anything but trash." She reached for his hand. "I think it bothers me now more than it used to because Stake's shown me what it feels like to be treated like I matter."

Tiny opened his mouth, but before he could speak, she held up her hand. "I know it probably won't last between us, so if that's what you're going to warn me about, don't bother. I'm not stupid. I know a man like Stake could have any woman he wants. He's with me because he feels guilty about what happened, and I think he has a misplaced sense of loyalty to take care of me because of my father."

"You're so full of shit," Tiny cut in. "I don't think you realize what he's willing to do for you. Leaving Broken Ridge is a big move for him. If the Fayetteville chapter doesn't accept him, he'll be a man without a club. If that happens, he'll no longer be allowed to wear his cut and he'll have to remove his Kings' tat. For a brother, that's huge." He cupped her cheek so tenderly it almost made her cry. "That's not loyalty, squirt, that's love."

She lifted her cup to her mouth and held it there for several moments as she considered the prospect of Stake being in love with her. He'd said the words earlier, and she'd accepted them because they made her feel good, but she hadn't genuinely believed them. The thought of him giving up his club for her started an ache in her chest. "He can't give up the club. It's his life."

Tiny shrugged. "I doubt you can talk him out of it, especially after what happened yesterday." He took another nip from his bottle. "I'm leaving for Oklahoma City tomorrow with Magic and Hog. There's some trouble with a rival club, and they've asked for our help. I don't know how long it's gonna take, so I might not be back before you leave."

She blew out a breath and reached for the whiskey. "You're telling me this may be goodbye, aren't you?"

He nodded. "I hope to finish in time to make the ride to Fayetteville. It's always a good party when all the chapters get together, and this year, you'll be there."

After taking a drink, she passed back the bottle. She hadn't confided her fears about moving to Arkansas to Stake, but she needed to tell someone. "What if..." She tried to swallow the lump of emotion that was slowly cutting off her air supply. "What if it's not just Broken Ridge that sees me as worthless?"

"Huh?"

Crap. She tried again. "What if I move to Fayetteville and they treat me like the people here have always treated me? Maybe the problem is me and not everyone else."

"Fuck," Tiny growled, throwing the near-empty bottle as far as he could. "This motherfucking town." He shook his head. "This town doesn't know where to put someone like you. Everyone's so busy trying to lump people into categories that when they get to you, they're lost. You're by far the prettiest, sexiest woman in Broken Ridge. Unfortunately, you've beat yourself up for so many years that your self-confidence is shit. People beat you down because they know they can get away with it. There's not a goddamn man in town that wouldn't love to fuck you, and every wife and girlfriend knows that."

Although in her heart, she didn't believe Tiny, she loved him for seeing the best in her.

"And as far as Stake?" He chuckled. "He's the meanest bastard in the club, when it comes right down to it, but I've seen the way he treats you, and if I hadn't witnessed it, I never would've believed that lion could be tamed."

Santana blushed. "Thank you," she whispered, reaching for his hand again. "Do you think you could visit us more than just once a year? I'm sure my ego's going to need regular doses of Tiny to get me through."

He lifted her hand to his mouth and kissed it. "Now that I have you back in my life, there's no fuckin' way I'm going to let you go again."

* * * *

Stake had no doubt Cecil wanted to discuss the confrontation he'd had with his mom, but no amount of talk was going to rebuild that bridge. He found Cecil, Hog and Magic seated in their usual spots around the large table they used for club business. He stopped in the doorway and stared at Hog and Magic. "I wasn't aware we'd have company."

"Sit," Cecil ordered.

Stake took his chair as far from the others as he could get. "I know I have two weeks left on our agreement, but in light of what happened yesterday in town, I'd like to get Santana out of here as soon as possible."

The three men exchanged glances. "That's what we want to talk to you about," Cecil replied. "The girls are having a fit, and disgruntled whores don't make as much money. We need you to stay a while longer. If you want to send Santana to Arkansas, do it, but we need you here."

"No," Stake refused. "We had a deal. I'll ride out the two weeks I have left and keep Santana at the house, but I'm not staying."

Cecil narrowed his eyes. "Are you challenging me?"

Stake knew he needed to tread lightly, but he wouldn't back down. "I'll find someone the whores will be happy with, but as soon as that's done, I need your word that you'll let me go, *and* you'll put a call in to Digger on my behalf."

Cecil scowled, but before he could say anything, Stake continued. "Smash saved your life and it cost him his own. Getting Santana the hell away from Broken Ridge would clear that debt."

Stake could tell by Cecil's expression that he didn't like being reminded of the debt he owed Smash for killing the cop, but a debt was a debt.

"The girls have to be satisfied," Cecil finally replied.

"They will be," Stake promised. Tiny was the first person who came to mind, but he wouldn't give Cecil a name until he discussed it with his friend. He left the clubhouse and found Tiny and Santana laughing their asses off. He stopped and drank in the sound of Santana's happiness. After everything she'd been through, he hated to pull her away from Tiny. As he crossed the distance between them, a plan began to form.

Chapter Nine

By the time Stake carried Santana to the pickup, she knew she was shit-faced. "I shouldn't have drunk that whiskey."

Stake smiled over at her as he climbed in the truck. "You're not planning to pass out on me, are you?"

"Nope." She giggled. "Although," she began as she hiked up her short dress, "you could keep me awake while we drive home."

With a deep groan, he unzipped his jeans. "Come closer, babe."

She licked her lips as she slid across the seat. "I love your cock," she slurred as she reached for him.

When she leaned down to plant her face in his lap, he grabbed her hair. "Touch me with those gorgeous fuckin' lips, and I'll explode."

She looked up at him. "I thought that's what you wanted?"

He shook his head. "My dick wants to be buried inside your pussy."

Score. She knelt on the seat and pushed her dress higher before moving to straddle his lap. The steering wheel bumped against her spine, but it wasn't enough to deter her from riding her man. "I love it when you talk dirty to me," she confessed, lowering herself onto his cock. She moaned as the bulbous head stretched her inner walls, sending sparks of pleasure through her body.

"Fuck, babe," Stake groaned. He squeezed her bare ass and lifted her up before letting her sink back down.

Each time he repeated the action, his fingers moved closer to her asshole. She'd become accustomed to his anal play while they fucked, but he'd never taken it beyond a finger or two. On more than one occasion, she'd almost asked him to take her there, but she'd always been too embarrassed to admit she wanted it. With the booze coursing through her blood, however, her inhibitions fell away.

"When are you going to fuck me there?" she asked when his finger penetrated her.

"Soon," he growled, pumping his finger in and out of her ass as he continued to fuck her pussy. "It'll take patience. I'll have to go slow with you, and I can't because every time you're naked in my arms, all I can think about is fucking your cunt."

She braced her hands on his shoulders and took over, riding his cock as fast as the tight confines of the pickup allowed. She wanted all of him. Every drop of seed, every look, touch and ounce of love he could spare for her.

Panting, she threw her head back. "I'm close."

Stake's entire body went rigid and she thought he'd come, but when she looked at him, his focus was on the road off to the left.

"Stop," he told her, lifting her off him.

When he set her on the seat, she groaned in frustration. "What the hell?" God, she'd been too close to be denied. She reached for her pussy to finish herself off when Stake stilled her hand.

"Cops," he warned as he stuffed his length back into his jeans.

Her attention snapped to the line of police vehicles speeding toward the parking lot with lights flashing. Oddly enough, their sirens weren't blaring. "What's going on?"

"I don't know." He reached over and helped her pull her dress down. "Whatever it is, it's not good." He eyed the hidden compartment where he kept his gun.

"No," she warned.

Stake met Santana's gaze. "I love you," he whispered as the police surrounded the pickup.

"What have you done?" she asked. Dammit, she'd wanted to kill Gordon before Stake had a chance to get to him.

* * * *

"Get your hands up in the air where we can see them!" a deep voice shouted.

Still staring at Santana, Stake tried to figure out what the hell was going on. It wasn't the first time the local cops had tried to make a bust at one of the club gatherings, but they didn't appear to be after anyone but him. "Say nothing, but do what they ask," he ordered as he raised his hands into the air.

Santana nodded and lifted her arms. "I love you," she said as their doors were thrown open.

Stake was jerked from the truck and pushed to the ground. The gravel bit into his body when three of the cops fell on top of him. What the fuck? He wasn't even resisting. "What's this about?" he demanded.

One of the cops wrenched Stake's arms behind his back. "Motherfucker!" Stake yelled when the cop pinched the skin of his wrist with the cuffs. "What the hell is going on?" He tried to turn his head to find Santana, but a knee against the side of his face kept him in place.

Cuffs in place, two cops jerked Stake up by his arms. "You're under arrest for the murder of Peter Gordon," one of the local cops hissed in Stake's ear.

The blood drained from his face as the charge sank in. He hadn't killed Gordon. *Fuck.* He frantically searched the growing crowd for Santana. When he spotted her, bile rose in his throat. Robby had her pressed against his patrol car, running his hands slowly up her bare thighs. "Langers!" he screamed as he fought against the cops holding him.

Robby turned his head and grinned at Stake as his hands disappeared under the short hem of Santana's dress. "Just frisking her," Robby yelled back. "Doing my job."

With her forehead rested on the hood of the car and her arms handcuffed behind her, Santana's entire body shook with wracking sobs. *Oh. God.* He fought again, knowing Robby's treatment would send her back to the night of her attack. "No!" he screamed as he kicked out against the men wrestling him to the ground.

"Help her!" he shouted to the crowd of brothers witnessing the event.

A kick to his ribs knocked the breath out of him as a punch landed against the side of his face. Never had he felt so goddamned helpless. Tears filled his eyes as he continued to stare at the love of his life.

A SUV pulled up, siren blaring. It cut off with a chirp as Jack Boone climbed out of his vehicle. Stake prayed the Texas Ranger would help Santana. When Jack made his way toward Stake, Stake shook his head. "Santana!"

Jack stopped and glanced around, his gaze finally landing on Santana. "What the fuck!" he yelled, marching over to Langers. He pushed Robby away from Santana and immediately pulled out a set of keys to release her from her cuffs. With a nod to Stake, Jack turned Santana around and pulled her against him. He spoke to her, but they were too far away for Stake to hear what was being said. It didn't matter to him. All that he cared about was keeping Langers away from her. He stopped fighting the cops and laid in the gravel, his entire body on fire from the blows and scrapes it had suffered while trying to get to Santana.

Jack wasn't perfect, but he was the best cop Stake had ever come across. He hoped he'd use his power to make sure Santana was treated fairly. As he continued to watch Jack soothe Santana, he couldn't help but worry that she had something to do with Gordon's death, but how was that possible? Since picking her up at the store the previous day, Santana hadn't been out of his sight except for the few minutes he'd been in a meeting with Cecil.

Jack walked Santana to his SUV and opened the door for her. He spoke to her again as he gently helped her into the backseat. After shutting her inside, he walked toward Stake. "Who's in charge?" he asked.

"I am," Buz Reynolds, the Broken Ridge Chief-of-Police, said as he stepped forward.

Jack put his hands on his hips. "I'd suggest you control your men before this crowd steps in to do it for you."

Stake noticed Tiny standing a few feet from Jack's SUV. With his hands fisted at his sides, Tiny stared at Santana through the darkened window. *Tiny?* He remembered Santana being unable to find Tiny earlier in the evening, and at that moment, Stake knew Tiny had killed Gordon. The timing had been absolutely perfect because Stake and Santana both had alibis. Oh, shit. He fucking owed Tiny his life for what he'd done.

* * * *

As he sped his way toward home, Stake continued to watch the rearview mirror for any sign he was being followed. The police had kept him and fourteen other brothers who'd tested positive for gunshot residue on their hands and clothing for over five hours while they'd questioned them over and over again. Each time Stake had made the same statement. He'd been at the party all evening and hadn't left the premises. Fortunately, he had close to fifty people who could corroborate his story. The same could be said for the rest of the brothers who tested positive.

Of course Jack and the other Rangers who'd shown up knew one of them was lying, but they couldn't pin the crime on any one of them. Stake was under no illusion that they would stop looking for answers and evidence of the shooting, but for now, they'd been forced to let them go with a warning not to leave town.

He pulled into his driveway and slammed on the brakes before jumping out of the truck. Hog's wife, Birdie, had taken Santana home soon after Jack had determined Santana's hands were clean.

As soon as he entered the house, Birdie jumped to her feet. "She's in the bathroom. I can't get her to talk to me."

Stake nodded. "Thanks for staying with her. I'll take it from here." He entered the master bedroom and knocked on the bathroom door. "Hey, babe? Can I come in?"

Nothing. Bile rose in his throat at the thought of her suffering alone for hours. He prayed she hadn't done something stupid. He rushed to the kitchen and retrieved the ice pick from the drawer before running back to the bathroom. It took only a moment for him to pop the lock and open the door.

Santana sat in the tub with her bent legs pressed against her torso. Arms wrapped around her legs, she rocked back and forth, seemingly unaware of his presence.

Within minutes, he was out of his clothes and prepared to join her in the tub. When his foot hit the water, he jerked back. "It's fucking freezing," he admonished, flipping the lever that would drain the water.

He teetered between lifting her out of the tub and joining her. In the end, he decided there had to be a reason she had climbed into the water in the first place. He began to refill the tub with warm water as he moved to squeeze in behind her. She still hadn't spoken, but she did turn to her side and rest her cheek against his chest. "Talk to me, lady bug."

"Why?" she asked.

He tried to hold her shaking body as close as he could as he willed his body to warm her. "Why what?"

"I was supposed to kill him. Why'd you do it?"

Stake blew out a long breath. He hadn't spoken of his suspicions to anyone, including Tiny. "I didn't. I was with you, remember?"

She looked up at him for the first time since he'd entered the bathroom. "Then who?"

"I don't know for sure, but I bet it was someone who couldn't stand the thought of that man living another day to torment you." Knowing how far Tiny would go for Santana had changed Stake's mind about asking Tiny to take over with the whores. He still wasn't sure how he was going to do it, but he needed to get Tiny transferred to Fayetteville, and that would be more easily accomplished if Tiny never slipped into the role Stake was vacating. He found the wet washcloth on the side of the tub and began to wash the smeared mascara from her face. "Whoever it was must love you a lot."

Her eyebrows drew together for a moment before shooting up to her hairline as the answer dawned on her. "Tiny?"

Shrugging, he grabbed the bar of soap and rubbed it against the washcloth. "Promise me that you'll never ask him about it. Believing he did it and knowing the truth are two different things as far as the police are concerned." He kissed the top of her head as he began to wash her chest. "Will you tell me why you were sitting in an ice cold bath?"

Tears filled Santana's eyes. "He touched me. Inside of me," she admitted as she turned her head away.

"Shhh. Don't cry. God, please, don't cry." No matter what he'd done in his life, nothing cut him like the sight of her tears, but she'd always had that effect on him. Until he'd met the young girl with kaleidoscope eyes, he'd never known what unconditional love meant. He'd survived his own childhood with an occasional pat on the arm or thank you, but had never heard the words he hadn't known he'd been missing until Santana had wrapped her skinny arms around his neck and told him she loved him when he'd brought her a Christmas present when she was barely five.

Those simple words had started to change the way he'd looked at himself in the mirror. His feelings of protectiveness had only grown once Smash had started the whippings. The first time he'd found her bruised and crying, he'd sworn to himself he'd make Smash pay for what he'd done. Unfortunately, Smash hadn't seen it the same way. He'd informed Stake that Santana wasn't his to worry about, and if Stake continued to try to insinuate himself into their family business, he'd make sure Stake never had contact with Santana again. Caught between wanting to help and the knowledge that he needed to be accessible to Santana in case the unthinkable occurred, he'd shut his mouth. And, with each beating, he'd lost a part of himself. By the time Smash had gone to prison and Ellie had made it impossible for Stake to look after Santana, the beautiful creature was no longer a child. He'd taken what was left of his self-worth and had sealed off his heart out of preservation.

"I feel dirty," Santana whispered, pulling him out of his thoughts.

"No, babe, you're not dirty, but let me wash Robby's touch from you." He soaped the washcloth again and tried to soothe the only person he'd ever loved. "Do you remember me taking you to the fair when you were little?"

She nodded.

"Those memories are some of the best for me. I loved hearing you laugh as you rode rides that you probably had no business being on. You were so fearless." He rested his cheek against the top of her head before tipping her chin back to press his lips to hers in a gentle kiss. "You still are. I admire the woman you've become even if it breaks my heart that you did it without my help."

"You're wrong." She rested her hand on top of his and pushed the washcloth toward her pussy. "There's nothing to admire about what I've become."

Although he knew she needed his touch, he wanted to shake her at the statement. "How can you say that? Look at you. Despite everyone in your life trying to knock you down, you're kind and loving, and so fucking perfect."

He acquiesced and ran the washcloth over her pussy several times. "You give me a reason every day to think before I act. In those years after your dad's death, I walked around without a soul. No job was too dangerous, because I didn't care if I lived or died. To be completely honest, there were times when I thought dying would be the best thing that could happen."

Santana pulled the washcloth out of his hand. "Let me feel you," she signed. "I need your touch to erase his."

He realized words weren't what she needed, and slipped his fingers between the lips of her pussy. She was slick and warm and he wished he could swallow her whole and protect her from the outside world. The house Gypsy had found for them was a step in the right direction, but he needed to make sure he only surrounded her with people who saw her as he did. That meant getting her the hell away from Broken Ridge. Unfortunately, until the investigation into Gordon's death was closed, he wouldn't be allowed to follow her.

"I need you to do me a huge favor," he said, slipping two fingers inside her core.

"Anything," she said, her breathing picking up.

"I can't leave town until I'm cleared by the cops, but I need you to go to Fayetteville and set up a house for us. My friend, Gypsy, found something, and it would really help me out if you could look at it and do whatever needs doing while I'm stuck here."

Before he had a chance to react, Santana pulled out of his grasp and stepped out of the tub. *Fuck!* "Babe, it'll probably just be for a month or so."

She spun around and glared at him. "I knew you'd leave me again. I thought I was prepared for it, but I didn't count on you sending me away."

"Goddammit!" Stake stood and climbed out of the bath. Without thought, he grabbed her upper arms and held her in place. "I fucked up when Smash died. I'm sorry that I abandoned you, but that's never going to happen again." He pulled her against his chest. "I'm nothing without you, and I mean that literally."

Slowly, as their skin began to dry, Santana returned his embrace. "You're my strength. I don't know that I can go through this without you."

Although he didn't believe it for a second, his heart filled to bursting. "I know you can do this, babe. I have to send you away or risk killing every person who tries to make you feel less than you really are."

She pulled away enough to stare up at him, but didn't say anything.

"I hope Fayetteville will be a fresh start for both of us. I want you to find girlfriends to laugh and gossip with because your happiness means more to me than anything else. And, while you're away, I trust Gypsy to make sure you have everything you need. He's a damn good man." He brushed his thumb down her cheek. "He even offered to take out Gordon for me, so I have no doubt you'll be safe with him."

"Is he married?"

Stake couldn't help but laugh. "Nope and according to him, it'll never happen. He's too fucked up because of his childhood, even worse than me, if you can believe it. Still, he's a good guy, and I promise he won't try anything with you."

"I'm not his type?" she asked, a glint of humor in her eyes.

"You're every man's fucking type, babe, but Gypsy knows how I feel, and he'll respect that." He didn't have any reservations about entrusting Santana to Gypsy. That wasn't to say she might not fall for the charismatic biker, but he hadn't lied to her when he'd said he wanted her to be happy.

"Okay," she finally agreed. "I'll go."

Chapter Ten

Spread eagle on the center of the bed, Santana buried her hands in Stake's hair as he ate the hell out of her pussy. Since Gordon's death two days earlier, Stake seemed intent on keeping her naked and at his mercy. She hadn't argued, knowing all too soon she'd be sent away.

"Yes," she moaned when he began to suck on her sensitive clit. It had taken hours of lovemaking for her to get over the hurt of being sent to Arkansas without him, but she'd come to understand that he believed he was doing the right thing. She wasn't sure she agreed, but with Robby still on suspension from the police department, he was a wildcard that Stake didn't need to worry about. If she stayed with Stake, there was no doubt he'd feel the need to protect her twenty-four hours a day, and he still had business in San Antonio that he needed to take care of before Cecil would let him transfer.

"You taste so fuckin' good," Stake growled, moving to kneel on the bed.

When he made a gesture for her to roll over, she quickly did as instructed. Dare she hope he would finally give her what she'd been begging for? Without embarrassment or reservation, she planted her knees and forearms on the bed and stuck her butt into the air. "Please?"

Stake ran his tongue up the crack of her ass before swirling the tip around her puckered hole. "Be patient. We still have at least an hour before Gypsy gets here." He reached into the bedside drawer and removed a bottle of lube.

She held her breath. He'd used it on her before but only with a finger or two, and she couldn't help but to wonder if she was truly ready for the feel of his cock in such a tight opening.

When he slowly began circling her hole with the pad of his lubed thumb, she moaned.

"Relax, babe. Lay your head down on the pillow, and let me have you," he said soothingly as he added more lube. "Deep breaths," he urged, working two fingers inside her.

It was the first time he'd started with two, and her body tried to protest the invasion. "No. Deep breaths, remember?"

She closed her eyes and tried to concentrate on her breathing as he pumped his fingers in and out of her. They'd discussed the process many times over the last few weeks, and she knew the first time would probably hurt before her body got used to his size. It had been the same with his cock in her pussy the first few times, so she didn't doubt she'd become just as addicted to his dick in her ass once her body accepted him.

Several minutes later, he kissed her spine. "I'm going to try another now," he warned before easing a third finger into her.

For some reason, the third was easier to take than the first two, and she was soon squirming for more. "Now," she begged. "Please?"

Stake withdrew, and within moments, she felt the head of his cock against her. "Ease back as much as you can."

She started to rise up again, but he stopped her with a hand to her back. "Relax. Just take a deep breath, and rock back onto me. Take as much of me as you can handle without too much pain."

Doing as instructed, she felt his crown press against her but not penetrate her. She tried again, putting more force into her actions and sucked in a sharp breath when she felt the head of his dick push inside her. "Oh, God," she panted at the burn. She started to retreat, but Stake grabbed her hips and kept her in place.

"Just wait. As soon as the pain stops, take a little more," he urged.

Like always, he was right. Within moments, the pain had dissipated, and she was ready for more. They repeated the process until his length was fully buried inside her.

"I feel a lump in my throat, and I'm afraid it's you," she said in an attempt to break the tension between them. She could feel his hold on her hips getting tighter and tighter the longer it took for her to fully accept his length. She knew he was dying to let loose and fuck her freely, but he was trying to spare her the pain it might cause.

With a grunt, he eased his hold. "I'm going to slide out and back in. You'd better fuckin' tell me if I hurt you."

She prepared herself for pain, but wasn't prepared for the loss she felt when he pulled almost entirely out of her. She wanted to scream in protest, but before she could open her mouth, he eased back inside. "Again," she moaned, experiencing nothing but pure pleasure.

He withdrew a few inches before pushing more forcefully inside. "Okay?"

"Uh huh." She hugged the pillow under her head as he started to fuck in and out of her.

With each pump of his hips, Stake groaned. "I'm not gonna last. Touch yourself."

As close as she was to coming, she wasn't sure she needed the added stimulation, but she did as asked, plunging her fingers into her pussy while her thumb centered on her clit. She felt the flutter in her stomach first before her body jerked as the vibration of her climax worked through her, leaving even the hair on her head tingling in ecstasy.

"Christ!" Stake bellowed as he bucked against her ass, his fingertips biting into her skin.

He slowly withdrew before collapsing onto the bed beside her. His breathing was erratic as he threw his arm over his eyes. "Never been like that," he panted.

She rolled to her side and moved to press against him. "Is that bad?"

He shifted his arm above his head and opened one eye to look at her. "For my heart? Hell, yeah." He grinned. "You've officially erased all memories of sex before you."

She'd always tried not to think about the hundreds of women who had been with Stake in the past, but it hadn't been easy. Hearing that she made him feel better than any other woman soothed the jealous viper within her in regards to the line of whores who'd come before her. A worry niggled at the back of her mind. "Will you be able to go without until we're together again?"

Stake leaned up on his elbows and gazed down at her. "You don't ever have to worry about me touching another pussy. Got it?"

She bit her lip, knowing easy sex was part of the biker lifestyle. "I can't say it would be a deal breaker for me if it happened, but I'm not sure my heart would recover."

Gathering her into his arms, he pulled her on top of him. "You've taught me something no one else ever has. Sex is hollow with the wrong person. Without you, the act of fucking doesn't interest me in the least. Not anymore."

The comment warmed her. "I love you."

* * * *

"He's here," Stake announced, opening the back door.

The glass she'd been washing broke as her hand involuntarily fisted at the words. *Shit.* She pulled her hand out of the dishwater and watched as blood began to run down her fingers. Leaving Stake was the hardest thing she'd ever been asked to do, but she'd tried to convince herself that it was what he needed.

"Fuck, bug, what'd you do?" He grabbed a dishtowel and cradled her hand in his palm as he examined the cut.

She didn't say anything, couldn't answer him for fear that she'd beg him to let her stay.

"Knock. Knock," a deep, graveled voice said from behind her. "Hope you don't mind that I'm early. Tiny had something he had to get to."

"Hey, Gypsy. Do me a favor and grab the first aid kit under the sink in the hall bathroom."

Gypsy walked over and peered over her shoulder before whistling. "That looks nasty."

"Yeah," Stake agreed. "The kit?" he reminded.

"Right." Gypsy left the kitchen.

"Talk to me," Stake demanded.

"I'm fine," she mumbled, refusing to look at him. Not only was Stake sending her away, but Tiny hadn't even cared enough to come inside. When Stake had told her Tiny was the brother who'd pick Gypsy up at the airport, she'd been relieved that she get a chance to see her old friend before she left. Wishful thinking.

"Bullshit." With a sigh, he led her over to the table and sat in his favorite chair, pulling her onto his lap. "It won't be for long. I promise."

She nodded. It wasn't the first time she'd heard the words. The goddamn tears started again as she remembered the last time he'd told her he'd be back. It had been one of the hottest summers on record and Stake had stopped by the house on his way out of town. He'd explained that he needed to help his brothers in Oklahoma City for a while and had stressed how important it was that she lay low with Smash while he was gone. He'd made her swear that if she noticed her father drinking she'd find somewhere else to go. Of course, she'd promised, she would have gone along with anything he'd wanted back then. He'd given her a kiss on the cheek and had told her it wouldn't be for long and he'd be back before she had a chance to notice he was gone. A day later her father had been arrested, and she hadn't seen Stake again until the time she'd been sunbathing and he'd stopped by Gordon's. The pain she'd felt that day still scarred her heart.

A white plastic box landed on the table, making her jump. Stake tried to soothe her with a kiss to her temple, but when he tried to wipe the tears from her cheek, she turned her head, knowing there'd only be more to replace them.

Gypsy pulled out a chair and started to sit, but Stake stopped him. "Why don't you load Santana's things while I get this cut taken care of?"

Gypsy didn't answer immediately, prompting Santana to look at him for the first time since he'd walked into the house. She was immediately taken with how much the two men resembled each other, same coloring, same dimples. She glanced at Stake. Same unusual amber-colored eyes rimmed in long black lashes. *No way.*

"Don't ask," he whispered in her ear.

"You okay?" Gypsy asked her.

She looked up at him once again and shrugged. Lying was the last thing she felt like doing. "It doesn't really matter, does it?"

Gypsy glanced at Stake before crossing his arms. "I'm not about to take an unwilling woman across state borders."

"It's not that," she said. "I told him I'd go."

"Would ya give us a fuckin' minute?" Stake asked.

"Sure. Are the boxes on the porch it?"

"Except for her suitcase, and I'll get that," Stake replied. "I'll pack up the rest of the stuff and bring it with me, but there should be enough there to make her comfortable."

Gypsy walked out of the house, leaving her to face Stake's temper. She knew she'd angered him, and she hated that she was acting like a brat, but it hurt knowing it could be months before she saw him again.

Stake opened the first aid box and removed a bottle of peroxide. He rested her hand on the dishtowel and poured the bubbling liquid over the cut. "Sending you away isn't what I want—far from it. But it's not safe for you here right now. I need you to understand that—not just agree to it."

Hiding her face with her free hand, she struggled to keep her emotions under control. "I'm sorry. I know I'm making this harder than it needs to be, and I know I'm being irrational, but I have this overwhelming feeling that I'm not going to see you again."

Stake didn't say anything until he'd finished bandaging her hand. Once her injury was taken care of, he led her into the master bathroom. "Sit," he instructed, pointing to the closed toilet lid.

She sat, trying to work out Stake's mood. He didn't appear to be angry, but his jaw was set, and he hadn't met her gaze.

Stake removed a screwdriver from under the sink before pushing back the bathmat on the floor. He knelt and pried up several floorboards before setting the screwdriver aside. Reaching inside, he came back out with a large duffle before setting it at her feet. "There's three hundred and twenty thousand dollars in there. It's every penny I've saved and what I plan to retire with. I want you to take it."

"I don't want your money." She pushed the bag toward him with her foot.

"I want you to use it to put money down on a house and to help furnish it with whatever we need. I'm pretty good with my hands, but if the place needs electrical or plumbing work, have that hired out." He slid across the floor to kneel at her feet. Wrapping his arms around her waist, he laid his head in her lap. "That money is my future. I wouldn't give it to you if I didn't plan to spend the next seventy years with you."

"Okay." What else could she say to something so heartfelt? "I'm afraid to go without you, but I'll try to feel better about it."

"You still have no idea how strong you are, do you? I'm glad you want to be with me, but you've proven to both of us that you're more than capable of taking care of yourself until I can get there." He sat up and kissed her, sweeping her mouth with his tongue, slowly and deeply. "Gypsy will be there whenever you need him."

"Are you related to him?" she asked. She couldn't figure out why he'd put so much faith in Gypsy when he rarely seemed to trust people.

"Probably, but we don't discuss it. We're not blind, we know we look alike, that's how we became friends. I went with the club to the big biker and barbeque weekend in Fayetteville and we ran into each other. That was twelve years ago and we've talked at least once a month since."

"Do you think you have the same father?" she asked.

"Who the fuck knows. Neither of us had a dad who stuck around after the party was over, so without tests, there's no way to tell."

Smash might have been a sick asshole but at least he'd cared enough to stick around. She'd never stopped to compare Stake's childhood to her own. It was obvious he had issues with his bitch of a mom, but had he been alone, or had he had someone like she'd had him? "Who did you go to as a child when you needed help?"

He seemed surprised by the question. His eyebrows drew together as he sat back on his heels. "When I was a boy, Cecil, I guess, but that changed once I told him I wanted to join the club."

"He didn't want you to?" She assumed Cecil would have been thrilled to have Stake follow in his footsteps.

"Cecil's..." He ran his fingers through his hair. "Cecil's life is the club, and when I became a prospect, he sat me down and told me he was no longer my uncle. That if I was going to become a member, I would have to understand that he was the prez." He shrugged. "I think that's why I started hanging out with Smash. Your family wasn't perfect, but it was the closest I'd ever seen at that point in my life."

She knew she needed to be more understanding. They were both carrying years of emotional baggage. "I think we still have a lot to learn about each other."

He pulled her off the toilet and into his lap. "Yeah, time apart might be good for us. We can talk on the phone, and I won't be able to get distracted by your beauty."

She felt so much better, but there was one thing still bothering her. "Why's Tiny avoiding me?"

"He's not," Stake denied.

"I need to know the truth. Does he regret doing what he did? Does he hate me now?"

Instead of answering her, Stake reached into his pocket and pulled out his phone. He scrolled through his contact list before hitting enter. Handing Santana the phone, he nodded. "Talk to him, but under no circumstances are you to discuss Gordon's death over the phone."

"You think someone's listening?" She couldn't imagine the investigators would go that far.

"I doubt it, but better safe than sorry."

"Hey. Is she gone?" Tiny asked.

She swallowed around the lump in her throat. "Not yet," she answered.

"Shit. Santana. I'm sorry, I thought it was Stake."

"Yeah, I got that." She leaned against Stake's broad chest. "Are you mad at me?"

"No. Why in the hell would you think that?"

"You didn't care enough to come in with Gypsy and tell me goodbye, so I guess I need to know whether or not you're happy that I'm leaving."

Tiny didn't say anything right away. Instead, he cleared his throat several times. "I love you, Santana, and the last thing in the world I want is for you to go away, but Stake's right, it's not safe for you here." He coughed. "Anyway, I guess I'm a chicken shit coward because I couldn't bring myself to say goodbye."

"I love you, Tiny. Will you come and visit?" she asked. Although he'd only been in her life again for a few weeks, they'd fallen right back to being friends, and she knew in her heart he'd done what he had out of love for her.

"Sure, as often as I can," Tiny replied.

She thought she detected a sniffle, but she'd never call him out on it. "I'll phone you when I get to Fayetteville."

"You'd better. Bye, squirt."

"Bye, Tiny." She hung up and handed the phone to Stake. "Thank you."

He nodded, stuffing the phone back into his pocket and gave her another deep kiss, squeezing her tight. "Time for you to get on the road. It's a long drive to Arkansas."

She climbed to her feet, feeling better, but still not happy about leaving. He shouldered the duffle with money before reaching for her hand. She let him lead her through the bedroom, where he grabbed her suitcase.

"Is there anything else?" he asked, looking around the room.

She thought of the gift she'd left under her pillow. It was her first attempt at drawing a self-portrait, but she didn't have a current picture to leave with him. She supposed she could have taken one on her phone, but there was something special about holding a real picture you couldn't get from a photo on a cell. "I think that's it."

He walked her out to the loaded pickup. "Take care of my girl," he ordered Gypsy.

Gypsy took the suitcase from Stake and fit it into a tight opening in the bed before reaching for the duffel.

Stake shook his head. "This needs to go behind the seat." He gave Gypsy a pointed look as he handed it over.

"What'll you do now?" she asked, wrapping her arms around his waist.

"I talked to Mad Dog about taking over for me with the girls. Corrine's not too happy about it, but I reckon she'll change her mind when she realizes he'll bring home a hell of a lot more money. Plus, I told him I'd sell him the house for below market if he'd take over. Corrine definitely wants out of his single wide, so that helped sweeten the deal."

She pressed her cheek to his chest and squeezed as tight as she could. "I took your cologne, by the way. You won't need it, but I will."

Stake tilted her chin up for a deep kiss. "I only have eyes for you," he told her.

Gypsy started the truck. "We need to get on the road if we're going to make it before dark."

Her heart sped up at the announcement. She stared up at the man she loved. "Call me every day."

He shook his head. "Morning, noon and night," he corrected. He pulled away enough to open the passenger door. "You shouldn't have any trouble with the truck, but make sure you always have your phone on you when you leave the house."

"I will." She climbed into the pickup and let him shut the door. Leaning out of the window, she opened once more for his searing kiss, hoping the taste of him would last until they were together again. "Love you," she whispered.

"Love you more." He pounded the roof of the truck. "Keep her safe," he told Gypsy.

"Will do." Gypsy backed out of the drive slowly. "You'll be fine."

When he pulled out onto the country road, she turned in her seat and waved, watching Stake as long as she could. With a sigh, she turned around and reached for her seatbelt. "How long is the drive again?"

"Nine hours or so. Depends on how often we have to stop." He grinned. "You're not one of those women who have to stop and pee every hour, are you?"

"I don't know. I've never been farther than San Antonio," she answered honestly.

Those amber eyes stared at her for several seconds before going back to the road. "In that case, feel free to ask me to stop whenever you see something that interests you." He winked. "We'll make a traveler out of you yet."

Approaching the interstate onramp, she spotted a lone figure leaning against a black Harley. "Oh my God." She reached for Gypsy's arm. "Stop."

As soon as the truck was pulled to the side of the road, Santana jumped out and ran toward Tiny. "You came!" She launched herself at him, knowing he wouldn't let her fall.

Tiny caught her against his muscular chest and swung her around. "I couldn't do it," he whispered in her ear. "I couldn't let you leave knowing it might be the last time I ever get to hold you."

She felt tears burn her eyes. "I know what you did." She kissed his cheek. "As soon as you're cleared, move to Arkansas with us."

"I can't move to Arkansas. What Stake's doing is special on account of you." He eased her back down to the ground. "But, if I make it out of this thing without getting caught, I'll make that drive whenever you need me."

She reached up and cupped his face in her hands. "I will always need you."

Chapter Eleven

A few miles outside of Fayetteville, Santana could no longer hide her excitement. "It's so green," she said in awe. Everywhere she looked were varying shades of green in the trees, the grass, and the plants. "It's beautiful."

Gypsy grinned at her. She'd caught him doing that a lot on their drive, but she didn't get a creepy vibe from him, more like he thought he was constantly indulging a child. She wondered if he thought she was too immature for Stake.

"In another week or two, the leaves will start changing. I can't wait for you to see it. It's quite a sight to behold," Gypsy casually said.

"I can't wait." She continued to stare out of the window. The drive had been exciting, and Gypsy had kept true to his word and had stopped each time she'd asked. She looked at the small snow globe that rested on the dash of the pickup. She'd found it in one of the souvenir shops they'd stopped at and knew it would be the perfect addition to Stake's Harley collection.

"It'll be too late to see the house tonight, but I've booked you a room in a motel not far from my place. I've already talked terms to the realtor. The house is empty, so as soon as the banks are ready to close, the place will be yours and Stake's." He glanced at her. "It's going to need a paint job inside and out, and if it were me, I'd have the floors refinished before moving in."

Santana had no idea what those things would cost. Although Stake was planning to bring the best pieces of his furniture, they would still have so many things to buy. She hated the thought of spending his savings and vowed to use as little as possible. "I'll talk to Stake about it once we know how much money it'll take."

They rode in silence for several miles before she noticed Gypsy looking at her again.

"What?" she asked. It was the first time since they'd started the drive that she felt uncomfortable.

"Nothing." He shook his head. "He used to talk about you," he mumbled. "I'm not gonna lie, I never understood why he tortured himself over the situation." He winced. "But, I get it now. Just thought you should know that."

Curious, she prodded for more information. "What did he tell you about me?"

Gypsy turned his attention back to the winding road. "It wasn't so much that he told me about you. Your name just seemed to come up in nearly every story he told. I always wondered what hold the girl with kaleidoscope eyes had on him." He gripped the steering wheel tighter. "It tore him up when he was ordered to stay away from you." He flicked his glance her way. "I hope you realize that. He even talked about going nomad over it, but I convinced him that his life would be nothing without the cut. I was wrong," he admitted. "So very wrong."

She took a moment for his words to sink in. Knowing that Stake hated not seeing her helped ease some of the hurt from the past. She didn't blame Gypsy for convincing Stake to stay with his brothers. Hell, she knew what going nomad meant, and she couldn't imagine him living his life without a family of brothers. "I'm glad you talked him into staying. Being a biker is who he is."

"It's good that you understand that."

She stared at Gypsy longer than she should have. Except for the shorter hair, she could almost convince herself that it was Stake driving the truck. It was disturbing and comforting at the same time. "You should grow a beard," she suggested.

He took a hand from the wheel to rub across his heavy five o'clock shadow. "I've grown one a time or two, but it takes more work to keep it up than to shave every day."

She bit her bottom lip, wondering how truthful she could be with the man. She wouldn't tell him that she didn't like beards so the distinction between him and Stake would be even more apparent if he grew one. "It would better suit your name," she finally said.

He chuckled. "Should I get a big hoop earring, too?"

"I'm sorry, I didn't…"

"It's okay." He reached over and squeezed her shoulder. "I know why you want me to grow a beard. I was just fuckin' with ya."

"You do?" Had she been so obvious?

"You're afraid of being tempted by my stellar looks, right?" he asked, with a wide grin on his handsome face.

"I'm not tempted," she snapped. "It's just that when I look at you, it makes me miss him."

"Relax. I was trying to rile you up. I know where your heart is." Gypsy made a left hand turn and pulled to a stop in front of a small but well-kept motel. He sat there for several moments without making a move to open his door. "My brother's a lucky man," he said before climbing out of the truck.

It was the first time he'd referred to Stake as his brother, and she wasn't sure if he meant the obvious familial connection between the two or the club connection. Either way, it was obvious he had honest feelings for Stake. The realization made her feel much better.

* * * *

"It's perfect," Santana gasped as she threw open the passenger door. The pale yellow farmhouse was set at an angle from the row of trees that hid it from the road. Gypsy had warned her that it would need some fixing up, but she couldn't see any imperfections in the two-story house. The wide front porch looked out over a small pond that, although overgrown with grass and cattails, would be spectacular once cleaned up.

She nearly floated toward the unruly red climbing roses that grew on a trellis attached to the side of the house. "It's so much prettier than the pictures you sent."

Gypsy moved to stand next to her. "The place has sat empty since February, so it'll take a fair amount of cleaning up, but it's a damn good buy."

She spun to face him, tears burning her eyes. "Can we see the inside?"

He pulled out a set of keys. "The realtor dropped these in my mailbox this morning. I think it's safe to say he's excited about selling the place. He wanted to come and give you a proper tour, but I told him you'd want to explore on your own."

"Thank you." She took the keys before making her way to the front porch. Stairs. She grinned as she climbed the five steps to the tongue-and-groove porch, making a mental note to remind Stake to bring the porch swing with him. God, she wished Stake was with her to see it. That in mind, she pulled the phone out of her pocket.

"Hey, lady bug," he answered on the first ring.

"It's beautiful," she said before filling him in on what the yard and house looked like on the outside. "I'm getting ready to go inside, but I wanted to hear your voice."

"I love the drawing," he told her. "I haven't got shit done today because I can't tear my eyes off it."

"I'm glad you like it. I didn't want you to forget what I look like." She smiled to herself as she thought of him sitting on the edge of the bed with her portrait in his hands. "I wish you were here to see the house with me."

"Tell you what. I'll close my eyes and you can describe everything to me. It'll be almost like I'm with you."

Her heart melted. He always seemed to know how she felt without her having to tell him. "Okay." She unlocked the front door and pushed it open. Looking over her shoulder, she called out to Gypsy. "Are you coming in?"

He shook his head. "Not this time. You go ahead."

Smiling, she stepped inside. "Oh," she gasped.

"What do you see?" Stake prompted.

"A staircase at the back of the entryway. It goes up about ten steps and there's a small landing before it makes a ninety-degree turn and continues. I'd like to put a plant there because there's a window right above the landing."

Stake chuckled. "Okay, babe. What else?"

She turned to her right and peeked into what appeared to be a formal dining room. "A dining room with horrible wallpaper, but it has molding around the top. It's pretty." She walked through the dining room to the kitchen. "Oh, Stake, the kitchen is huge, and there's a big old table that would probably seat ten people." She ran her hand over the table. It had to have been built in the room because there was no way it would have fit through the doorway. "It needs to be sanded, but I can do that."

"What about the rest of the kitchen? From the pictures, it looked like it would need some work."

"The cabinets appear to be solid wood, so they can easily be stripped and stained or repainted." She opened one of the cupboards to see how deep they were and screamed.

"What's going on?" Stake asked, his voice full of worry.

"Sorry. It's okay. Just a dead rat." She heard the front screen door bang shut moments before Gypsy came running into the room.

"Are you okay?" Gypsy asked.

She nodded and pointed to the decomposing houseguest. "Sorry. I didn't mean to scare you. I wasn't expecting it."

"Gypsy?" Stake asked.

"Yeah." She felt her face flush. "I think I scared him more than I did you."

"I doubt it," Stake grumbled.

She was surprised by his reaction. "Is everything okay there?" she asked.

"You're not here. Of course, everything isn't okay," he practically growled.

It was on the tip of her tongue to remind him that he was the one who'd sent her away. Her good mood from earlier began to dissipate. The line was quiet while she watched Gypsy use a piece of cardboard to remove the rat.

"Are you alone?" Stake asked.

"No," she answered.

"Find the master bedroom," he instructed. "I'll wait."

"Bedrooms?" she asked Gypsy.

"Three up and one down," he informed her, pointing to a short hallway off the kitchen. "The one down is right through there, but it's small and doesn't have an attached bathroom."

"And the master?" she asked.

Gypsy shook his head. "It doesn't really have one. The three rooms upstairs are all roughly the same size and share a single bathroom."

With the phone still pressed to her ear, she followed Gypsy's directions to the first floor bedroom. She was surprised at its size, although the proximity to the kitchen wasn't ideal. "For now, I think we should use the downstairs bedroom for us. That way, we can shut off the upstairs. Once we have children, we can move up there to be close to them."

"Kids?" Stake questioned.

She silently cursed herself. Stake had never mentioned getting married or having a family. "Well, you know, if we eventually decide to have them."

"Maybe," he answered. "Whatever you decide is fine."

She wasn't sure if he was referring to the bedroom situation or the children, but she let it go. She opened the small closet and noticed further evidence of vermin. "I think we'll need an exterminator."

"Have Gypsy set it up," Stake ordered, his voice still gruff.

She finished the rest of the tour with less enthusiasm. "Well, that's it," she said as she walked back out to the porch.

"Is it the house you want?" he asked.

"It's the house of my dreams," she answered honestly. "But, I'll be happy anywhere as long as you're with me."

"I need to go, but tell Gypsy to call me after he drops you off."

"I will." She was still kicking herself for mentioning children. Had she ruined everything?

"I miss you," he said.

The warmer tone to his voice helped soothe her racing heart. "I miss you, too."

"Call me before you go to bed tonight," he ordered.

"I will." She hung up and clutched the phone to her chest.

"Everything okay?" Gypsy asked.

"I don't know. I hope so." She held up her phone. "He wants you to call him after you drop me off."

Gypsy narrowed his eyes as he watched her. "Okay."

* * * *

By the time his phone rang, Stake was in a foul mood. The conversation with Santana earlier had left a bitter taste in his mouth. Gypsy's overt display of concern for her had really pissed him off, which didn't make sense since he'd been the one to ask Gypsy to care for her. His anger went beyond normal jealousy. It felt like he'd ripped out his heart and had handed it over to another man. Once Gypsy had pulled out of the drive with Santana beside him, it had taken everything Stake had not to get on his bike and chase them down. Santana's place was beside *him*, not Gypsy. Santana's mention of having children had totally knocked him on his ass.

He had no doubt Santana would make a good mother, but he was a selfish bastard who'd waited too long to have her. Sharing her with anyone else didn't set well for some reason. He'd heard the stories from his brothers on how their wives had changed after giving birth. He liked having Santana ready and willing to fuck anytime he asked and wasn't about to give that up without a fight. Besides, he didn't think he had it in him to be a good father, and he'd lived a life of subpar parenting. How the hell could he willingly take a job like that on, especially knowing how fucked up his own childhood had been? Yeah, he was definitely a selfish prick, but he refused to mess up a kid like his parents had done with him. Babies should be protected from the worst of life, and he associated with the dregs of society on a regular basis. Shit! He wanted to give Santana the world, but he'd never wanted children. The problem was, what if not having babies was a deal breaker for her?

He dug the phone out of his pocket. "Hey," he answered.

"What's up?" Gypsy asked.

"See if you can fax the paperwork on the house to the club. Cecil's called a meeting later, so I'll swing by the club early and have plenty of time to get the paperwork signed and sent back before church."

"All right." Gypsy sighed. "Mind telling me what you said to Santana over the phone that upset her?"

"Don't fuckin' worry about what I said to my woman. We're good." Once again, Stake was second guessing his decision to send Santana to Arkansas without him. Gypsy was almost as bad as Iggy when it came to sex. How many times had he watched Gypsy pick up a stranger in a bar and fuck her against the wall within five minutes of meeting her? Not that he hadn't had his share of quick fucks, but Gypsy seemed to need it every motherfucking day whether he had a girlfriend or not.

"I am going to worry about it. She walked into that house with the biggest smile I've seen out of her yet and came out looking like she'd been kicked. She didn't say a goddamn word on the drive back to the motel."

"I'm not sure I like where this is going. I asked you to watch over her, not crawl up her fuckin' ass. If you need pussy, get it from somewhere else." Stake gripped the phone so hard he was surprised the damn glass didn't shatter in the thing.

"You sonofabitch!" Gypsy growled. "When I came down to Texas to pick her up, I couldn't fucking believe you'd twisted yourself up so much over a fucking cunt, but after spending hours with her alone in the truck, I got it. Now, I'm wondering why the fuck she'd do the same thing over a bastard like you."

"Fuck you," Stake barked. "She's my fuckin' life, and I'm not about to lose her to you." He was seconds away from jumping on his bike and going to Santana when he heard Gypsy's laughter. "What the fuck's so funny?"

"You," Gypsy replied. "You're so goddamn jealous, you don't even trust her."

"I trust her," Stake argued.

"Evidently not, or you wouldn't be afraid of me making a move on her, which I would totally do if I didn't care about you, asshole. But I do care, and I wouldn't do something like that."

"Just send the fuckin' papers." Stake hung up before he said something else he'd regret.

* * * *

Santana picked at her salad. She was grateful Gypsy had come back into town to take her to dinner, but she wasn't good company. "Did the realtor say how long it would take?" she asked, searching for something to say.

"Two weeks minimum. You have to have an inspection, and then there's all the bank paperwork." He shrugged. "Takes a while." He ate another bite of his burger. "The repairs to the house will probably take another week, at least. Will you be okay in the motel that long? I'd offer you my spare bedroom, but I think Stake might slit my throat for that."

She grinned for the first time since her phone call with Stake earlier in the day. "Don't take it personally. He's jealous of Tiny, too, and I've never had a sexual attraction to Tiny."

Gypsy paused in the process of lifting a fry to his mouth. "Are you telling me you're attracted to me?"

Shocked at what she'd said, she dropped her fork and covered her mouth with her hand. It wasn't that she thought of having sex with Gypsy, but there were times when she looked at him and could convince herself it was Stake at her side. Several times, she'd barely caught herself before reaching for his hand as they walked through town or rode in the truck. When he'd pulled up in front of the motel on his Harley, she'd adamantly refused to ride on the back of his bike because she wasn't sure how the proximity would affect her. They'd ended up walking to the restaurant because she'd told him Stake wouldn't like the thought of her on someone else's bike.

"It's understandable if you are. It doesn't make you a bad person. I know how much Stake and I look alike."

She shook her head. "It's not that I'm attracted to you, it's that I'm attracted to the parts of Stake that I see in you," she said.

"It's the same thing," he argued.

"No, it isn't." She was starting to get angry. "I love Stake."

"Right, but you think he's sexy, therefore, it would only make sense that you think I'm sexy, too."

When she noticed the mischievous smirk on his face, she groaned. "Are you fucking with me again?"

"Yeah," he admitted. "You're fun to tease."

She picked up her fork and began eating. "You can be a real bastard."

He chuckled. "That's what they tell me."

* * * *

Two and a half weeks later, Santana stared at her packet of birth control pills with dread. Her period was late. At first, she hadn't given it much thought, believing the new prescription had messed with her cycle, but it had been eight days and still nothing.

Stake had made his feelings quite clear on the subject of children, and whether she wanted to admit it or not, their differences of opinion had affected their relationship. She'd been so busy simply trying to survive before Gordon attacked her that she hadn't considered the possibility of a husband and children. It hadn't been until she saw their new house that she'd begun to truly believe in a future with Stake. Naturally, marriage and children were the next step in their relationship. Boy, had she been wrong.

Although she'd tried to broach the subject several times over the phone, he'd shut down each time she mentioned it until she'd convinced herself that she could have a full life with him regardless of whether or not they had children. She sank to the bed.

She had no idea how long she'd stared at the wall before a knock sounded at the door. Sick at heart, she stood and unlocked the door for Gypsy.

"You ready?" he asked, excitement in his voice.

It was to be their third day to work on her and Stake's newly purchased home. "Almost," she replied, refusing to look at him. She hadn't cried much, but Gypsy always seemed to pick up on her distress, similar to the way Stake did. She grabbed her purse. "I need to stop by a drug store on the way if you don't mind?"

"Don't mind at all." He blocked her exit before she could get out of the room. "What's going on? You and Stake have another argument?"

She shook her head. "I'm fine."

"No you're not." He crossed his arms over his chest.

Telling Gypsy about her period wasn't an option. "I just wish Stake were here to help us," she lied.

"Soon." Gypsy started to reach for her but dropped his hand. "You sure that's all?"

"I'm sure." She plastered on a fake smile. "I'm ready."

* * * *

Eying Jack's SUV, Stake parked in front of the club. He'd only spoken to the Texas Ranger twice in the three weeks since Gordon's murder and still couldn't get a read on how the investigation was going. Stepping inside the club, he was surprised when the usual blast of hard rock didn't assault him upon entering. He spotted several brothers sitting around the room with worried expressions.

"What's going on?" he asked the prospect who was tending bar.

"The Ranger's in a meeting with Prez. You want something to drink?"

"Beer's fine." Stake turned on his stool to stare at the closed door of the meeting room. "Any indication of what it's about?"

The prospect sat a bottle in front of Stake and shook his head. "They've only been in there for about ten minutes."

Tiny got up from the table he'd been sitting at and joined Stake at the bar. "How's Santana?"

Stake nodded without taking his eyes off the door. "Good. We got the house, and she's been working on the yard." He didn't tell Tiny that things between him and Santana had been strained since the discussion of children. As hard as he'd tried, the idea of sharing her with anyone else simply couldn't excite him. Tiny was different because Stake could always tell him to take a hike if he wanted to be alone with his woman, but he couldn't do that with kids, especially when they were little.

The door opened and Jack walked out alone. "Be right back," Stake told Tiny as he crossed the room. "Any news on when I'll be cleared to move to Arkansas?"

Jack motioned for Stake to follow him out of the club. Once in the parking lot, Jack headed for his vehicle. "The investigation has officially been put on the back burner. We know someone in this club is guilty, but we don't have a strong enough case against anyone to press formal charges." He opened the door to his SUV. "You have an address in Arkansas yet?"

Stake nodded. "We just closed on a house outside Fayetteville."

Jack pulled a small pad of paper out of his pocket and handed it to Stake along with a pen. "As long as you let me know if this address changes, you're free to go." He leaned his forearm against the door. "I know why you sent Santana away, but I have to tell you, it looks suspicious."

Stake handed Jack the pen and pad. Staring him straight in the eyes, he answered, "I did not kill Pete Gordon. I'm not sorry he's dead, but I didn't do it."

Jack continued to study Stake for several moments before giving him a sharp nod. "I'm glad to hear that." He glanced at the address and phone number Stake had scribbled down before climbing behind the wheel. "Good luck to ya."

"Thanks." Despite being on opposite sides of the law, Stake respected the Ranger. He went back inside the club and clapped Tiny on the back. "We're good. They're shelving the investigation for now due to lack of evidence."

Tiny let out a long breath. "Thanks for telling me."

"Church!" Cecil yelled from the meeting room doorway.

"You planning to bring up your transfer?" Tiny asked as he finished his beer.

"Hell, yeah. Mad Dog's adored by the whores, so getting the okay from the cops was the last roadblock between Santana and me. Can you get away for a couple of days to help me move?"

"I don't know. I'll have to ask Cecil because I've already scheduled time off for the Bikes, Blues and Barbeque thing next month," Tiny replied. "If I can get both weekends, I will, but otherwise, pussy and barbeque has to win out."

Chuckling, Stake pulled out his phone. "Go on in, I'm gonna give Santana the good news before I have to drop the phone off." He hated the strict no phones in church policy, but it had always been that way. When her voicemail clicked on, he groaned. "Hey, it's me. Thought I'd call before things get busy. I'll try ya again later." He set his phone on the table outside the meeting room along with all the others, excited by the notion he'd be with her within a day or two.

* * * *

After a hot shower and pulling on one of Stake's old T-shirts, Santana climbed into bed. The combination of a full day of yard work and the positive pregnancy stick on the bedside table left her a snotty, sobbing mess. Although she'd somehow managed to stop crying, she had no doubt her eyes would be swollen in the morning. She picked up her phone and called Gypsy.

"Everything okay?" he answered. It had taken him four rings to pick up and from the sound of the bitching woman in the background, Santana had a pretty good idea what she'd interrupted.

"Sorry to bother you. I'm pretty sore, so if it's okay, I think I'll sleep in tomorrow." She rolled to her side and brought her knees up, curling into a ball.

"It's fine. I can run by and get the floor crew started. No problem." He didn't say anything more, and she was about to hang up when he finally sighed. "You've been crying."

And, just like that, the dam broke again. She'd spent the majority of her life refusing to give into tears, so where had her willpower gone when she needed it the most?

"Santana? What's wrong, hon?" Gypsy asked, sounding incredibly worried.

"I'm pregnant," she managed to say between sobs.

"That's good news. Why the hell're you crying about it?"

"Because Stake doesn't want kids," she confessed. "I didn't mean for it to happen, and now I don't know what to do."

The woman in the background said something Santana couldn't hear but she definitely heard Gypsy's response to her. "Then get the fuck out, bitch." He cleared his throat. "Sorry about that, Santana."

"I should let you go," she said, drying her tears. "I'll figure this out somehow."

"What is there to figure out? You have to tell him."

She knew Gypsy was right, but how could she? Stake had already given her more than she'd ever dreamt of, asking him to care for a child he didn't want would be pushing their relationship too far.

"Santana," Gypsy growled into the phone. "You have to tell him."

"I know, but what if..." She couldn't finish the sentence, couldn't even think of living without Stake.

"Don't," Gypsy warned. "Don't borrow trouble. Tell him. Don't automatically assume you know how he's going to react. That's not fair to him."

"Okay. I'll call him right now." She blew out a breath. Gypsy was right. She had to get it over with and deal with the fallout afterward. "Thanks for listening."

"Call me after you talk to him. I've run off my pussy for the night, so I'm not busy."

"I will." She hung up and started to call Stake when she noticed he'd left a message while she'd been in the shower. She quickly listened to the message before calling.

"Hello?" a sultry voice answered.

Santana pulled the phone away from her ear and glanced at the display to make sure she'd dialed the right number. "Is Stake there?"

"He's in the shower. Is this Santana?"

Santana swallowed the bile working its way up her throat. "Yes. Who's this?"

The woman let out a soft giggle. "Rachel. I've been meaning to thank you for leaving town. It's been so nice to have Stake back in my bed, and I just wanted to tell you, expecting him to come to your rescue like that was a really shitty thing to do to him. You used his loyalty to your father against him by tricking him into taking responsibility for you."

The breath froze in Santana's chest as she threw her phone across the room. It hit the mirror over the credenza and fell down the wall in pieces, cracking the mirror in the process. "Damn him!" she screamed as she jumped out of bed and ran to the bathroom. She fell to her knees in front of the toilet as her life fell apart.

Sometime later, she heard the sound of the room phone ringing but ignored it. She was too numb to move or speak to anyone. Nothing in her lifetime had ever hurt her more than knowing Stake had already replaced her. She couldn't help but believe that's why he'd been so distant on the phone lately.

She heard her door open and come up short with the rattle of the chain lock. "Santana!"

"Go away, Gypsy!" she screamed even though her throat felt raw.

"Open this fucking door before I break it," he warned.

It took her a few minutes to get to her feet. Once she was finally up, she forgot what she was doing until she heard a loud crack. She blinked several times, looking around the bathroom for the source of the sound.

"Santana," a soft voice said her name.

She turned to find Stake standing in the doorway. "You're here." She ran to him and wrapped her arms around him, burying her face against his chest. "Rachel told me you were in the shower. She said you were fucking her."

Strong arms wrapped around her, and she closed her eyes, happy it had all been a dream. She inhaled deeply as she always did when Stake held her. She froze when she smelled spice rather than citrus. Jerking back, she stared up into a face that wasn't Stake's at all.

"Gypsy?" She reached out for the vanity when her legs began to buckle, the horror of the phone call flooding back to her.

"Fuck," Gypsy said, sweeping her up into his arms. He carried her to the bed and gently laid her down before pulling the covers over her. He sat on the edge of the mattress and brushed her hair away from her face. "What the fuck happened?"

She stared up at Gypsy, willing her lips to move. "Rachel answered Stake's phone."

"Who the fuck's Rachel?"

"A pretty girl that Stake likes to fuck, evidently." She buried her face in the pillow. "I've been a fool. She told me that he was only taking care of me because of my dad. I should've known. How could I have been so stupid, so greedy?"

Chapter Twelve

After church, Stake hung back until the rest of the brothers filed out. He'd been given permission to transfer with the understanding that Mad Dog could handle the girls. "I just wanted to make sure you'll talk to Digger on my behalf?" he asked his uncle.

"Already done," Cecil said, getting to his feet.

Stake held out his hand, but Cecil surprised him by pulling him in for a hug. "I'm back to being your uncle now, boy," Cecil bellowed in his ear.

After nearly twenty years in the club, Stake wasn't sure how he could be expected to forgive everything Cecil had done and accept him as his uncle again, but he didn't want to do anything that would jeopardize his transfer. He patted Cecil on the back twice before pulling away. "I'm going to pick up a moving truck tomorrow. I should be out of here the morning after that. Can Tiny take a few days off to help me move?"

"Sure," Cecil agreed. He speared Stake with his gaze. "One more thing before you leave."

"Yeah?" Stake held his breath, wondering what hoop he needed to jump through next.

"Did you kill Gordon?"

"No, but I wish I had," Stake answered honestly.

"You know who did?" Cecil asked.

Stake didn't trust Cecil with that kind of knowledge. "Nope," he lied. He left the room and stopped off at the table to retrieve his phone, noticing he had three messages, all from Gypsy. His heart thudded as he listened to the first message.

"What the fuck have you done? Sananta's...fuck, I don't know what she is, man, but I've never seen a woman break down like she has. It's one thing for you to screw around on her, but you'd better tell that bitch of yours not to answer your fucking phone next time."

While he tried to work out the first message, Stake continued to the second.

"I'm worried. I don't know whether I should take Santana to the hospital or just wrap her up and take care of her my way. You'd better fucking call me, you bastard."

He started toward the door as he played the last message.

"How fucking long does a shower take, motherfucker? I finally got Santana to sleep, but I'm worried about what this is doing to the baby."

Stake stopped in his tracks. He rocked back on his heels as sweat beaded on his forehead. "What the fuck?" *Baby?* His heart started to race as he fumbled with his phone once again. He called Gypsy, something he should've done right away instead of listening to the string of incoherent messages.

"'Bout fuckin' time," Gypsy answered.

"What the hell's going on?" Stake asked, climbing onto his bike. He felt like his heart was about to beat through his chest. All he knew was he was leaving immediately to ride to Arkansas. Fuck his shit, nothing in his house was more important than Santana.

"Santana called you earlier, and your little whore Rachel answered. I still haven't gotten the whole story out of Santana, but evidently your piece of ass on the side really laid into her."

"I've been in fucking church for the last three hours, so I don't know what the fuck you're talking about as far as Rachel, and I really don't know what fucking baby you're worried about."

Gypsy sighed. "Shit. If you've been in church all evening then Rachel hijacked your fucking phone."

Stake wiped the sweat from his forehead as he glanced around the parking lot. His gaze landed on Rachel's sports car. "That fucking bitch." He climbed off his bike, intent on finding the cunt. "And the baby? What baby?"

"The one Santana's carrying. She's been crying all evening, wondering how she was going to tell you. That's why she called in the first place," Gypsy explained.

"And Rachel answered instead," Stake surmised. "Talk about a fucked-up mess." He threw open the door of the club. "I'm leaving here in thirty minutes or less. Expect me by morning."

Stake shoved the phone in his pocket. "Where's Rachel?" he asked the room.

The prospect pointed toward the back. "I saw her go back with Tiny after the meeting," he said, trying to keep his voice low enough that Magic didn't hear.

"Thanks." Stake walked down the hallway to the room Tiny often used to fuck his whores and opened the door without bothering to knock. Rachel was naked with her lips wrapped around Tiny's cock.

"What the fuck?" Tiny asked.

"Sorry about this." Stake grabbed a handful of Rachel's bleached blonde hair and yanked her head back. "You fuckin' bitch. How dare you fucking answer my phone and upset the mother of my child." He pulled her off the bed and toward the door.

"Let go of me!" Rachel screeched, scratching at his arms.

Stake gripped her hair tighter and twisted one of her arms behind her back as he pushed the naked slut into the main area of the club. "Where the fuck is Magic?"

"No!" Rachel screamed, trying to get away.

"Cecil's office," one of the brothers replied.

Without knocking, Stake opened Cecil's door and pushed Rachel inside. "I've never hit a fucking woman in my life, but I'm two seconds away from killing this one." He pointed at Magic. "Keep your slut of a daughter at home before she tries to break up more families."

"Daddy!" Rachel cried, running to stand behind Magic.

"What the hell's gotten into you?" Magic demanded. "How dare you put your hands on my daughter!"

"I fucking dare because she answered my phone while I was in church and told Santana that I was in the shower because we'd just fucked!" Stake shouted, his anger out of control. "Rachel's the biggest slut the club has. Ask her? Better yet, go out there and ask your brothers how many have fucked her in the last month?"

Magic turned on Rachel. "Is that true?"

Rachel had pulled a throw off the ratty couch and had wrapped it around her. "He used me," she accused, pointing to Stake.

Disgusted, Stake held up his hand. "I'm outta here." He gestured to Rachel. "That mess is for you to sort out."

* * * *

Only an hour outside of Fayetteville, Stake was forced to stop for gas. He filled up the tank before going inside to get a cup of coffee. He'd survived the night on adrenaline, but even that was starting to wane.

As he sipped his coffee, he wandered down the aisles, amazed at how much shit a person could buy at a truck stop. The sight of a miniature Harley Davidson T-shirt immediately caught his attention. He hadn't allowed himself to think about the baby. Anger and the eight-hour ride had made his mind cloudy enough without adding thoughts of a child to it. He still didn't know what he was going to say to Santana, but as he lifted the small shirt off the shelf and held it in his hands, the situation took front and center. It appeared he had no choice in the matter, because he wouldn't live a day without Santana.

He carried the coffee and the shirt to the register, knowing he had an hour to get used to the idea of becoming a father. How the fuck could he be a father when he hadn't had one of his own?

After tossing the dregs of his coffee into the trashcan, he carefully hid the shirt away in his saddlebag. An hour. Within the hour, if he pushed it, he'd be able to set things right. Gypsy had told him she was broken, but Stake refused to believe a simple phone call could break someone who'd survived the shit she had.

He roared out of the truck stop, intent on being there when Santana woke up. Although he appreciated Gypsy taking care of her, it was his face he wanted her to see when she opened her eyes, his arms that wanted to hold her while he told her the truth about Rachel, and his heart he wanted her to still need.

He rode into Fayetteville at seven-thirty, praying he'd made it in time. He texted Gypsy and asked for her room number as he paced back and forth in front of the motel.

A door opened, and Gypsy stepped out. He shut the door quietly before motioning for Stake to come over. "She's still out of it, but it doesn't surprise me."

"I need to see her," Stake said, trying to get around Gypsy.

"I told her the truth when she woke up crying earlier, but I don't think she believed me." Gypsy ran his hands over his short hair. "I don't know, man, I've never seen someone shut down like that. My guess is that everything's finally caught up to her. I couldn't understand most of what she mumbled about, but I clearly heard Gordon's name." He met Stake's gaze. "And Smash's."

Fuck. Guilt settled heavily on his chest. He should have known she'd bounced back from the attack and her mother's death too quickly. He'd gone on and on about how strong she was, and all the while, she'd simply buried it. If he hadn't hated himself before, he sure as hell did now. Fighting back tears, he nodded at Gypsy.

"I'll be at your place if you need me for anything," Gypsy said as he walked toward his bike.

Stake stared after his friend. While he'd cleaned up his shit in Texas, it had been Gypsy who'd taken his place with Santana. He wasn't sure whether to hate him or love him for it.

When he reached for the doorknob, his gaze landed on the splintered wood on the jamb. Between one breath and the next he was thrust back to the night of Santana's attack, back to the best and worst night of his life. He'd been so grateful to her for allowing him to take care of her that he'd willingly believed her when she'd claimed to be ready for the next step. He'd taken her to bed and had kept her there while she should have been dealing with everything that had happened.

Remembering the shirt in his saddlebag, he strode back to his bike and retrieved it. He didn't have the ability to go back in time to fix his fuckups, but he could learn from his mistakes and give her the life she deserved.

He opened the door and stepped inside, unsure of what he'd find. Santana was on her side, curled into a protective ball similar to the one he'd found her in the night of the attack. He was bone-tired from the hard ride, so he sat on the edge of the bed and took off his boots and vest. The Broken Ridge patches had already been stripped from his cut, but it still meant as much to him as it ever had.

Without bothering to remove his clothes, he slipped under the covers and pressed himself against Santana, molding himself around her frail body. He had no intentions of waking her, but he knew the moment she felt him.

Santana stiffened before relaxing and hugging his arms against her chest. "Thank you for being here," she whispered.

It was Stake's turn to go rigid, knowing she believed him to be Gypsy. The realization felt like a hot knife plunging into his heart. "Gypsy left," he whispered. "I rode all night to get to you."

Without turning around, she tried to pry his hands away from her body. He wasn't about to budge until he set things straight. "I was in church for hours last night. That's where I was when you called. Rachel must've heard my phone ringing and picked it up." He kissed her neck, praying he was getting through to her. "I would never touch another woman. I've had a lifetime of sluts like Rachel, and all of them together didn't satisfy me half as much as one kiss from you."

Her shoulders began to shake and he realized she was crying.

"Look at me, bug," he pleaded.

When she didn't make a move to roll over, he got up and went around to kneel next to her side of the bed. He rested his face on the mattress, willing her to open her eyes. "I love you. I wish I had the words to explain how deeply I need you, but I'm a fuckin' biker, so I'm going to try and put my feelings in a way you'll understand. The cut stands for my pride, my surrogate family, my self-worth, my career, my life. That piece of leather is everything I thought I ever needed, but I'd give it up right now if you asked me to, because I've realized that you're my cut."

Those gorgeous fucking eyes opened to gaze at him for the first time. "I'm pregnant."

He nodded. "I know, and I'm sorry I made it so you were afraid to tell me, but I need you to understand that it was never a child I didn't want." He dragged his fingers through his dirty, windblown hair. He swallowed around the lump in his throat. "I'm afraid of what'll happen to me if you love a child more than me. I'm a selfish prick, and I know it. I'm ashamed of the way I've acted, but I can promise that I'll love any and all children we have."

Santana leaned across the distance and gave him a soft kiss on the lips before pulling back. "I don't know that it would be possible to love anyone more than you." She bit her lip. "Every time I think of having a piece of you inside of me, it fills me with a feeling I can't explain. Just knowing that, no matter what happens, I'll always have that part of you in my life helps me not to be so afraid of losing you."

"You're not going to lose me." He'd tried so many times to make her understand that their relationship was the real deal for him. "I'm here now, and I'm not going back to Texas unless there's a damn good reason for it, and even then, I'll take you with me if that's what you want."

"What about the club and the investigation?"

"Taken care of. Cecil set me free, and Jack told me lack of evidence has the investigation stalled. He gave me permission to move as long as I kept him updated on my current address. Before going into church last night, I asked Tiny if he'd help me move."

"Tiny's coming?"

"Yeah. Although I need to call him. I kinda lit out of the club in a hurry last night." He wondered what Tiny's reaction to Rachel was after he found out what the bitch had done. There was a very good possibility that Rachel was history at the club, which was a damn good thing. With all the Kings of Bedlam chapters meeting up several times a year, it would be best if he never set eyes on Rachel again.

"I bought something on the way here." He stood and retrieved the T-shirt from the opposite side of the bed before crawling back under the covers with Santana. He held the shirt up. "It should work for a boy or girl, but I'm secretly hoping for a girl."

"That's surprising," she said, rolling over to face him.

"Not surprising at all. Boys will be boys, and they tend to need a heavy hand at times. I'm not sure I have it in me to do that, but a girl that I can spoil and treat like a princess? Yeah, *that* I can do."

* * * *

Santana stared at the outfit Stake had bought her the previous day for the Kings kickoff party for the Bikes, Blues and BBQ motorcycle rally in town. Was he kidding? She looked like one of the bitches from his motorcycle magazines. She pulled back the white bedroom curtain and bent over. "Ummm, Stake, can you come in here?" she called through the open window.

Stake was sitting under his favorite shade tree with Tiny, Gypsy and Gypsy's friend Mojo. He glanced up and smiled. "Be right there." He tilted back his beer and drained the bottle before heading for the back door.

She let the curtain fall back into place and waited. The dress made the one she'd worn to Mad Dog's wedding look downright matronly in comparison. The expensive black leather dress was skintight with a zipper that ran from hemline, which was almost short enough to expose her pussy, to neckline, which plunged low to reveal half her tits. It was an incredibly sexy dress, but one she didn't think was appropriate for her first big Kings' party since moving to Arkansas. She'd met several of the brothers' wives and girlfriends, but she didn't know any of them well enough to wear such a slutty outfit in front of them.

"Fuck!" Stake growled from the doorway. His hand immediately went to the front of his jeans to palm himself. He walked slowly toward her. "That body is begging to get fucked."

"No, it's the dress that screams 'fuck me I'm available'. Something I don't think you really considered," she argued as he began to lower her zipper.

"I like the fuck me part, but everyone there will know you're not available to anyone but me." He stopped when the zipper was halfway down and shook his head. "No bra." He unclasped her black bra, baring her breasts to his hands. He led her toward the bed and sat down, pulling her to stand between his legs. "I wanna know I have access to you at all times."

Her breath hitched when he sucked one of her nipples into his mouth. As he sucked, he lowered the zipper the rest of the way until the only thing holding up the dress was her shoulders. He shook his head, without releasing her breast, when his hands came into contact with her panties. Evidently, panties weren't necessary either, because he ripped them from her body with one tug.

She barely caught herself before she moaned when two of his fingers plunged inside her pussy. "The window," she tried to remind him.

Releasing her nipple, he grinned up at her. "I'm pretty sure they have a good idea of why you called me in here."

She braced her hands on his shoulders as his thumb began to rub against her clit while his fingers fucked in and out of her. "I called you in about the dress," she panted, riding the edge of climax.

His fingers stilled and he removed his thumb from her clit.

"Don't stop," she urged, trying to fuck herself on his fingers.

"Wear the dress, and I'll let you come." His voice was rough, and she could tell he was as turned on as she was. "Change, and I'll make you suffer all night before I get you off."

She reached for his hand, needing him to move those damn fingers again.

"No," he said, removing his fingers completely. "Choose."

"You're an asshole," she said, although there was no heat behind her words.

"Yes, a horny fucking asshole. What'll it be? You want my fingers, my cock or my mouth?" He flicked his tongue out just to tease her.

With her mind befuddled, there was no way she could make that choice. "Just make me come," she begged once again.

Unzipping his jeans, Stake pulled his heavy erection free. "Take it."

She was like a junkie in dire need of her next fix. Straddling his lap, she waited for him to fit the tip of his cock to her pussy before impaling herself on his thick length. "Mmmm," she moaned as the walls of her cunt stretched to accommodate him.

Grabbing a fistful of her hair, Stake devoured her mouth with a plundering kiss as she shrugged completely out of the dress. She opened and greedily took everything he offered. Never would she be able to get enough of him. Since moving into the farmhouse two weeks earlier, they'd made love so often they usually walked around without getting dressed. Stake hadn't been kidding when he'd said he needed access to her pussy at all times.

Breaking the kiss, he released her hair and grabbed her ass as he fell back onto the bed. She planted her hands on his chest and rode him hard, giving them both what they needed as their combined moans and grunts filled the room. "Touch me," she urged.

His calloused thumb rubbed against her clit as she continued to rock back and forth on top of him.

"You're so fucking sexy," he groaned, licking one of her bobbing tits as she moved. When he captured one of her nipples with his teeth and bit down gently, she gasped. Her orgasm rocketed through her body, stealing the breath from her lungs.

With a loud growl, he rolled them over and pounded his cock in and out of her pussy. Their couplings always turned into a primal mating that neither of them could control even when they tried to take things slow.

She felt another climax building as he drove into her. She knew he wouldn't stop until she'd come again because he prided himself on giving her twice as much pleasure as he took for himself. It was the way he went about everything where she was concerned. The phone conversation with Rachel had been devastating to her, but somehow Stake had used the episode to make their relationship even stronger. She'd even started to believe she deserved the happiness he promised. She cried out as another orgasm wracked her body, sending it jerking with the intensity.

"Fuuuccckkk!" he howled, drawing the word out for several seconds. He collapsed on top of her to the sounds of applause from the backyard.

Santana buried her face in his neck, mortified. "I'll never be able to look them in the eyes again."

Chuckling, Stake pulled out and held out his hand. "You'd better get over that quick, because we're leaving in five minutes."

She reached up to finger her hair. It felt like a rat's nest. "I can't go like this," she protested.

He picked up her dress before helping her into it. "Are you kidding? The just fucked look is breathtaking on you."

She rolled her eyes while he zipped her up, sans underwear or a bra. "If I wear this and it makes the other women hate me, I'll never forgive you," she pouted.

"Women will always be jealous of you, babe, but I think you'll be surprised because this dress, while sexy as fuck, is typical for this type of party."

"You'd better be right," she warned before racing into the bathroom to wash up and brush her hair.

* * * *

Stake stood with Tiny, Gypsy and Mojo, and watched Santana slowly make her way down the line of vendors. The party the previous evening had proved to him just how well they both fit in with the new club. Even Digger, the club's prez, seemed to take a liking to Santana within seconds of meeting her.

"Does she have to stop at every booth?" Tiny whined, growing impatient.

"Leave her alone," Stake barked. "Look at her." He couldn't believe how lovely she looked in the pale pink, floral maxi dress. It was vastly different from the sexy outfit she'd worn the night before, but no less perfect on her. She smiled and spoke to the vendors at each booth about whatever craft or items they were selling. He'd had a few doubts when they'd first moved to Fayetteville, but the longer they stayed, the more she seemed to blossom. "Did you ever think you'd see her smile like that again?"

Tiny sighed. "You're right," he conceded. "But if you're going to be here for more than a few minutes, I'm gonna get me another beer."

Stake waved off Tiny without tearing his gaze from Santana. "Do what you gotta do."

Santana was laughing with a gorgeous black-haired woman at a jewelry table. Santana turned toward him and held two necklaces up, shrugging her shoulders before teetering her hands up and down like Lady Justice holding her scales.

She was too far away for him to see the necklaces clearly, so he decided to brave the crowd. "Be right back," he told the others. He was still twenty yards away when a Scorpion MC member in a frayed denim jacket started talking to her. Santana shook her head and pointed in Stake's direction. When she tried to step away from the man, the asshole moved closer.

Stake wouldn't jump the guy, knowing that the Kings had a tentative alliance with the Scorpions, but he wasn't about to let the fucker make Santana uncomfortable. "You're a little close to my woman," he told the Scorpion.

"Don't see a ring or a vest on her," the Scorpion shot back. He was big, but not as big as Stake. The patch on his cut said his name was Top.

Stake thought of the ring he'd been waiting to give Santana when the time was right. He fully admitted to himself that he was nervous as fuck about proposing. It wasn't being married that scared him, but that goddamn proposal. He'd listened to enough old ladies to know they liked to compare stories on how their men asked the big question, and so far, Stake hadn't come up with shit.

"Well, I'm telling ya, she's mine. So now you know," Stake replied, wrapping an arm around Santana's waist.

Top grinned at Santana. "Is that the truth?"

She nodded. "I've already told you I was with someone."

Top tried to crowd Santana again, but Stake slammed his palm against the man's chest. "Back the fuck off," Stake said, quietly enough that the milling children didn't overhear.

"You need to educate your bitch," Top said. "Because being with someone and being a brother's woman are two different things."

Stake saw red. Even knowing that bitch was a common name for biker babes, he had never, and would never, call Santana that. Before he could control himself, he landed a punch to Top's jaw.

His head snapped back, but instead of going down, he retaliated with a punch of his own. Unfortunately for everyone involved, his fist grazed Santana's cheekbone before connecting with Stake's mouth.

Stake heard Santana's cry of pain and charged the motherfucker who'd dared lay a hand on her. He tackled Top to the ground, heedless of the crowd around them, and went fucking nuts. The two were in an all-out brawl by the time Gypsy, Tiny and Mojo stepped in to pull them apart.

"Not here," Gypsy growled in Stake's face.

Stake straightened his cut and swiped the back of his hand across his bloody lip. "He hit Santana."

Gypsy released Stake immediately, but Mojo was there to take his place. "I'm fine," Stake told Mojo, trying to shake the brother off. He held up his hands in surrender. Once he was confident that Tiny had control of Top, Stake turned to find Gypsy examining a small cut on Santana's cheek.

"Rain," Gypsy all but gasped at the sight of the pretty woman. He composed himself quickly. "Do you have a cooler back there?"

She nodded and wrapped several cubes of ice into the bandana Gypsy handed her. "Will she be okay?"

"I'm fine," Santana said, grimacing as Gypsy touched the makeshift cold pack to her cheek.

"I've got it." Stake had come a long way in admitting that Gypsy was his half-brother, thanks to Santana, but that didn't mean he was any less jealous of the bastard.

Gypsy stepped back and shoved his hands in his pockets. "Sorry about that," he told the woman he'd called Rain.

"It's good to see you again, Gypsy, but don't apologize. The asshole deserved that and more."

Santana took the ice pack out of Stake's hand and moved it to his lip. "You're hurt," she said.

"I've had worse." Stake glanced over his shoulder, looking for that sonofabitch again so he could fucking kill him. He spotted Tiny talking to another Scorpion and wondered where the hell Top had gone. Returning his attention to Santana, he redirected the cold pack back to her cheek. "I don't think it needs stitches, but we should find a drug store and pick up some butterfly bandages."

"I'm fine. Really," she repeated.

He placed his palm against her still-flat stomach. "The baby okay?"

With a smile, Santana pulled Stake's head down to whisper in his ear. "If this baby can survive the way you fuck, he can surely survive this."

"She," Stake corrected. He brushed her hair away from her face. The last thing he'd wanted was for her to experience violence in their new hometown, and the more he thought about it, the madder he became. "Let's get outta here."

"No," she refused. She still had the two necklaces clutched in her hand. "I'm buying one of these, then I'm going to continue to shop my way down this street. I was run out of one town, and I won't let that happen again." She held up the two necklaces. "Now, which one of these do you like best?"

Stake crossed his arms over his chest as adrenaline continued to pump through his body. "Get 'em both." He wasn't happy, but it wasn't her fault, and he be damned if he'd let his foul mood ruin her day.

Santana handed the necklaces to the woman. "I guess I'll take both of these."

* * * *

Santana collapsed on the blanket beside Stake. "I'm officially worn out." The evening was winding down as the sound of live music filtered through the air, creating the perfect end to an incredible day.

He rolled to his side and propped his head on his hand. Looking down at her, he touched his fingertip to the bandaged cut on her cheek. "It's bruising."

Staring up at him, she shook her head. He'd babied her all afternoon for the small cut when his injuries were so much worse. "I'm fine. How many times do I have to tell you that?"

"I guess until I believe it," he replied. He leaned down and kissed the injury. "I keep promising that I'll never again let someone hurt you, and then I fail to keep you safe."

"Stop," she said, covering his lips with her hand. She'd kept so many of her feelings bottled up, too afraid to make a fool of herself by speaking them aloud, but as she stared into those amber eyes that she'd always loved, she got the feeling he still didn't understand the way she felt.

"When I was a child, I loved you as that funny man who gave me piggy back rides and made me laugh. When I became a teenager, I loved you because you were the only man who showed me kindness and cleaned me up after Dad took his fist or his belt to me."

Stake closed his eyes, obviously upset by the memories of that period in her life. "And then I left you," he whispered, his voice thick with emotion.

She'd given a lot of thought to the period in her life when she'd felt abandoned, and had realized a few things. "I know you feel guilty about that, but I really need you to move beyond it because without those years spent on my own, I'm not sure what kind of person I'd be. They say that our pasts make us who we are, and for some unbelievable reason, I've grown into the kind of person a man as wonderful as you can fall in love with. Those years on my own made me stronger, but more importantly, they gave me an appreciation for the life you've shown me since the attack. Each time you make waffles for me or reach for my hand when you're asleep, I thank God that He brought you into my life. I don't need you to wrap me up and keep me safe from the outside world. I need you to be there for me when the outside world lets me down. There's a huge difference in the two, and I need you to understand that."

Stake leaned down and rested his forehead against Santana's. "I hear you, but I'll still do everything I can to protect you. I'd give my life for yours in a heartbeat because without you, I wouldn't want to live another day."

She wanted to argue, but how could she? He'd always been her protector. Asking him to stop now would be the same as telling him he was no longer needed. "I just want you to love me and continue to make waffles at least once a week."

He dug into his pocket and set a small opened black leather box on her stomach. "I've been trying for days to think of a way to propose to you. In my mind, it needed to be over the top in order to be special, but you've made me realize it's not about the process, it's about the outcome. Would you, Santana Elizabeth Rogers, make me the luckiest man in the world and marry me?"

Santana stared at the band of diamonds. She couldn't imagine a better proposal, and it had nothing to do with the engagement ring. For a brief moment, she considered telling him to take it back and get something more practical, but his pride in the band he'd chosen was written in his expression. Love for Stake, the ring and the promise he was asking her to make, filled her with joy. "Of course I'll marry you," she said, leaning down for another kiss.

Epilogue

Stake finished helping Tiny set up the chairs and shook his head. The warm, autumn day would be perfect for a wedding. He'd pushed to have the ceremony at the clubhouse because the weather in Arkansas was often unpredictable, but Santana had argued that they'd waited too long for their happily ever after to worry about things they had no control over. He'd wanted to point out that having the wedding inside was something they could control, but he'd quickly discovered it was best not to argue with a pregnant woman.

"Eighty, right?" Tiny asked, counting the rows.

"Yeah, that's what she said," he answered. He still couldn't believe his soon-to-be bride had insisted on inviting not only the brothers and their girlfriends and wives, but the whores he worked with. He liked most of the women, but he'd never have imagined Santana would want them at their wedding.

Once again, she'd surprised him by accepting the whores for the women they were. She had never once looked down on them for their profession. Instead, she'd made it a point to meet and talk with each of them. There were a few she didn't care for, but she claimed it was more personality conflicts than what they did for a living. When he'd asked her why she wanted them at the wedding, she'd told him it was to remind the girls that after today, he'd be a married man. He couldn't argue, although he'd told her repeatedly that hers was the only pussy he'd ever want. He liked the fact that despite getting to know the girls, Santana still had a jealous streak and wanted to publicly stake her claim.

The low rumble of a Harley caught his attention. He glanced to the front of the house and spotted Gypsy pulling to a stop in the driveway. Stake left Tiny to fuss over the chair placement while he greeted his best man. He'd laughed his ass off when Santana had informed him that she wanted Tiny to be her maid-of-honor. It had become even funnier once he'd told Gypsy that he'd be escorting Tiny down the aisle after the ceremony.

"All the work done?" Gypsy asked, climbing off his bike. He was dressed in black jeans, a white dress shirt and his cut, the same outfit Stake and Tiny would wear, although Stake told Tiny he'd have a pretty bouquet instead of a boutonniere. Predictably, that had earned him a fist to his jaw. It had been worth it.

"Just about," Stake answered. "I think Tiny's taking this maid-of-honor thing a little too seriously."

"Where's Santana?" Gypsy asked.

"At the salon. Rain's treating her to a bunch of beauty treatments. It's total bullshit, she's already gorgeous, but it's Rain's wedding present to her, so it's not like I could say no."

Gypsy ran his hands over his short dark hair. "That worthless husband of Rain's isn't coming, is he?"

Stake shook his head. "He's on the road." He'd only met Manny Silva once and that had been more than enough. Worthless was an apt description for the asshole. A long-haul trucker, Manny was only home one week a month, and according to Santana, Rain wasn't allowed to go anywhere or talk on the phone when he was in town. The one occasion Stake had met the fucker was right after Rain and Santana had become friends after talking at the Bikes, Blues and Barbeque rally. Manny had been in town that weekend and had made a complete ass out of himself when he'd shown up at Rain's jewelry booth soon after the altercation between Stake and Top. Stake would have sworn fear had flashed through Rain's pale green eyes when Manny had demanded to know how much money she'd made.

A few days later, Santana mentioned that when she'd met Rain for lunch, she'd noticed bruises on her wrists. It was something Stake had promised to keep an eye on. He liked Rain and was happy that Santana had found a girlfriend so easily, but putting Santana in danger wasn't an option.

A white compact car pulled into the driveway, prompting a smile from Stake. He walked over and opened the passenger door, pleased to see the hairdresser had left Santana's dark hair down.

"Hey. Hey. Hey," Tiny scolded pushing Stake back. "It's bad luck to see the bride before the wedding."

"We fucked all morning, and the day's been perfect so far," Stake growled.

Santana laughed. "Give me another hour, and I'll be all yours." She gave him a quick kiss on the cheek before running inside the house with Rain.

"Well, fuck." Stake stared at Tiny. "I thought you were her maid-of-honor, not her goddamn bodyguard."

"I am all things," Tiny replied. "Now, I'm going to crack open a beer and take my place on the porch so I can direct traffic once people start arriving."

Stake turned away from the lunatic and noticed the rage on Gypsy's face. "What?"

Gypsy pointed to the house. "You didn't see her?"

"That gorgeous woman who'll be my wife? Yeah, I saw her."

"Not Santana. Rain." Gypsy narrowed his eyes and climbed the porch steps, disappearing into the house before explaining himself.

"I'm surrounded by a bunch of crazy people," Stake mumbled as he walked back to the site of the ceremony.

* * * *

Santana shared a smile with Stake as she danced with Digger, the club's prez. Digger was an incredibly handsome man of around forty-five with short, salt-and pepper-hair. She didn't know his history, but she knew he wasn't married because he'd come to the wedding alone.

"Stake told me about the baby. Congratulations," Digger said. Despite his smile, she felt sadness radiate from him.

"Thank you." She leaned close enough to speak into his ear. "And thank you for accepting us."

"Don't thank me. Stake's a godsend with the girls. I had no idea what a difference one person could make, but profits are way up." He shrugged. "They're happy." He shook his head. "Hookers are never happy."

"Despite their situation, kindness and respect go a long way in helping a person feel good about themselves." She knew firsthand. "Stake understands that."

She felt a solid body press against her back and glanced up and over her shoulder. "Hey."

Stake grinned at her before turning his attention to Digger. "You're getting a little close to my wife."

Digger chuckled. "Jealous?"

"Wouldn't you be?" Stake asked, wrapping a proprietary arm around Santana's waist.

An expression of despair crossed Digger's handsome face. "Yeah." He took a step back before lifting Santana's hand to his mouth. After placing a soft kiss on her hand, he smiled. "Thanks for the dance."

"You're welcome." She watched him go before turning to drape her arms over Stake's shoulders. "I thought you said you didn't dance."

"I don't, but it seems I'm going to have to get over it unless I want to share you with every man here," he whispered in her ear, taking a moment to suck her lobe into his mouth.

"They're just being nice," she scolded. "I like them." She scraped her teeth across his shadowed jaw before asking the question on the tip of her tongue. "Why's Digger so sad?"

Stake drew her even closer and bent to bury his face against her neck. He placed soft kisses on her heated skin before moving to her ear. "He lost his wife about eight years ago. They'd only been married for a couple years when she got pregnant."

Her stomach flipped when she realized where the conversation was headed. "He lost them both," she said.

"Yeah," he confirmed. "But that's not gonna happen with us. Got that? So I don't want you to worry."

She wouldn't, but something told her he would. She pressed her cheek against Stake's chest and watched Digger refill his cup of beer. God. Her heart broke for him.

"I need to go," Rain said, touching Santana's shoulder.

Santana stopped dancing and looked at her friend. Rain was quickly becoming the best girlfriend she'd ever had, and she didn't like the distress she saw from the pretty woman. "What's up?"

Rain opened her mouth to speak, but Gypsy barged onto the dance floor and grabbed her upper arm. "We're not done talking," Gypsy growled.

"Yes. We. Are." Rain pulled out of Gypsy's grasp. She turned her attention back to Santana. "I didn't want to leave before I told you congratulations, and to remind you to call me as soon as the two of you come up for air in the next day or so."

Santana wasn't sure what had come over Gypsy. He was one of the gentlest men she'd ever known. When he started to reach for Rain again, Santana slapped his arm. "What're you doing?"

Gypsy glowered at Rain but spoke to Santana. "Did you even ask her how she got the cut on her lip?"

"Yeah," Santana answered. "She said she smacked it on the corner of the bathroom sink when she bent over to pick up her hairbrush."

"She told me she did it in the kitchen," Gypsy accused.

"Stop," Rain said, holding up her hand. "This is none of your business."

"The hell it isn't," Gypsy argued. "That sonofabitch put his hands on you, didn't he?"

"Stake, would you please walk me to my car?" Rain asked.

Stake released his hold on Santana and raked his fingers through his hair. He narrowed his eyes and darted a glance between Rain and Gypsy. "Sure." He pointed at Gypsy. "You stay here with Santana."

When Santana noticed Gypsy's hand curl into a fist, she quickly wrapped it in her hands, getting his attention. "Not today," she warned. "We'll figure it out, but this isn't the place."

Gypsy's jaws twitched several times before he nodded.

Santana leaned over to give Rain a kiss on the cheek. "I'll call you."

Rain nodded. She gave Gypsy one last pleading look before walking away with Stake right behind her.

Santana pulled Gypsy off the dance floor and to a quieter spot where they could talk without yelling. It wasn't the first time she'd noticed signs of abuse, but every time she'd tried to talk to Rain about it, her friend completely shut down.

"How can you just let her go back to that?" Gypsy asked.

"Manny's not even in town, so pushing her isn't the way to go." She knew from her own experience how humiliating it was to have other people witness the signs of a beating. "She's embarrassed, and we have to tread lightly, or she'll push us away."

Although his breathing was still ragged, Gypsy reached out and touched her cheek with his fingertips. The bruises had faded and the cut had barely left a mark, but he obviously remembered. "I don't understand a man who can hurt a woman."

"Neither do I," she agreed. "Rain told me you dated in high school." The information had floored her at the time, but it was plain to see how much Gypsy still cared for Rain.

"Yeah. Before I moved away for a year when we were seventeen. When I came back, she was with Manny," Gypsy explained. "I told her then that he was no good, but she wouldn't listen."

Santana wondered if Rain was the reason Gypsy never got emotionally involved with women. She wouldn't ask, of course, because it wasn't her business, but she couldn't stand to see two of the people she cared about most in pain. "Let me talk to her again and see if she'll open up. You barging in and scaring her isn't the way. Trust me on this, okay?"

"I want to kill him," Gypsy confessed. "Even knowing I'd probably get fingered for the job, I want to do it."

"And that's exactly the reason why you're going to let me handle this," she warned. She moved in to hug him. "For the first time in my life, I'm surrounded by people who care about me, and I'm not about to give that up without a fight."

He returned her embrace and kissed the top of her head. "Just promise that you'll do it quick before that asshole touches her again."

"I'll try." She wasn't sure how to make Rain understand that she didn't deserve to live a life afraid of someone who was supposed to love and protect her, but she'd find a way.

"Seriously, brother, I've already put a ring on it," Stake growled, pulling her away from Gypsy.

She sank back against her husband's chest as his hands settled on her still-flat stomach. His jealousy still didn't make sense to her, but she reveled in it each time he beat his chest and proclaimed to the world that she was his. Some might see the world she lived in as imperfect and often times dangerous, but she couldn't imagine any other life. She had everything she'd ever wished for. Her hands drifted down to cover his. And some things she'd never known she'd needed.

About the Author

An avid reader for years, one day Carol Lynne decided to write her own brand of erotic romance. Carol juggles between being a full-time mother and a full-time writer. These days, you can usually find Carol either cleaning jelly out of the carpet or nestled in her favourite chair writing steamy love scenes.

Carol Lynne loves to hear from readers. You can find her contact information, website and author biography at http://www.totallybound.com.

Home of Erotic Romance

www.ingramcontent.com/pod-product-compliance
Lightning Source LLC
Chambersburg PA
CBHW020407180626
46812CB00003B/871